TALES OF THE FORGOTTEN WORLD

Crystal Peake Publisher
www.crystalpeake.co.uk

This edition published in November 2018 by Crystal Peake
Publisher

www.crystalpeake.co.uk

Print I S B N   978-0-9935582-4-5
eBook I S B N   978-0-9935582-5-2

Text copyright © Kevin Peake 2018
Text copyright © Kathryn Popp 2018
Text copyright © Tarana Begum 2018
Text copyright © Alexandra Ispas 2018
Text copyright © Tomas Marcantonio 2018
Text copyright © Nisha Hamilton 2018
Text copyright © Danielle Adams 2018
Text copyright © Alex Stabler 2018

Cover © Crystal Peake Publisher 2018

A catalogue copy of this book is available from the British Library.

Typeset by Crystal Peake Publisher
Cover designed by T K Palad
Map designed by Renflowergrapx

Visit www.crystalpeake.co.uk for any further information.

Drakland

Waque

Fogvalor

Kai Darl

Ceat

The Forgotten World

Slay-Waterways

High Wilds

Tuskbane

Silane

Lastra

LANTRA OCEAN

CONTENTS

CÓLION
by Kathryn Popp

'Move it, Cólion! We've got an entire day of rounds to do!'

Cólion glanced up at Alred and snapped his small book closed, shoving it in his oversized boots.

'Sorry about that, sir,' he said quickly. 'I was wondering what the best weapon for today would be.'

Alred harrumphed and left Cólion, muttering about 'new generations.' Alred was kind but he had a habit of making his temper as short as himself.

At age seventy-three he had been injured during the start of The Great War, earning an early retirement after the bones in his left leg had been shattered. After that, Alred had built a weaponry for the elves of Waque.

One day, Cólion would make history; he would stop the drac's and maikong's. He would make them pay for fighting with the elves. Queen Canadiel's army would need every weapon that Cólion could make.

The dark elves; the drac's. The drac's were clever and fought dirty; winning every fight with the elves, they never went into battle without an unfair advantage.

The maikong's, on the other hand, no one knew much about. What they did know was that they were foxes with humanoid features; arms, legs, some even had fingers and toes. The maikong's always attacked in groups of four, yet they didn't use weapons.

But what made them so deadly, was the amount of casualties after an ambush.

'Cólion, we've got three steel swords and a shield, so start moving!'

Cólion jumped up and ran to a large silver anvil. Picking up his hammer in one hand and an iron rod in the other, he ran around his post looking for coal. Finally, he stopped and dragged some out from under a shelf. He would have to tell Alred that they would need more.

A few minutes later, Cólion was working fast, having already done two swords. Cólion hummed as he hit the hammer against the sword, keeping the rythm in touch with the hammer. After a few more hits, he was able to admire the sword. The blade was light and had a needle-thin point.

'Raid!' Alred shouted from outside. 'Cólion! Get out

now!'

Cólion dropped the sword and sprinted to the door before he froze and raced up the wooden steps. He dove to the side of his bed and yanked out a black satchel before heading for the stairs.

BOOM!

Cólion heard the loud explosion before he tripped over the steps.

The last thing he saw before he blacked out was the wooden floor rushing up at him.

****

Cólion squinted and slowly opened his eyes, a jarring movement causing him to wake up. Through his bleary eyes he made out bars. Metal bars.

Cólion's eyes widened in shock and he attempted to move away, only to find his hands bound tightly behind his back.

Cólion thrashed around in his small prison, trying and failing, to slip out of his bindings.

After a few minutes, he gave up.

Instead, he rolled onto his side and stood up, trying to get his bearings. Only to have his head thump on some sort of metal roof.

Cólion cursed and crouched on his knees, finally noticing that he wasn't just in a cell but a moving metal cell. He could hear the whip crack and strike horses, the laughter of the drac's and the wagon wheels turning over the gravel.

Cólion slumped over on his side. He wouldn't get out, that much was certain. He would be beaten and held unless the war stopped. But it wouldn't help the drac's or the maikong's.

No, Queen Canadiel wouldn't give in that easily. It would only enrage her.

Cólion smiled to himself, imagining elves marching in and ending the War themselves.

The sudden snap of a whip catching on his cheek made Cólion jerk back with a yelp before he heard the drac's cackle in delight.

'Hope you're cozy there, little elf!' One of them taunted before lashing at the cage again, the whip striking Cólion's arm and drawing blood. Another hit catching him on his leg, the gash was deep and flared with hot pain.

Cólion cried out as the drac's continued to laugh, whipping him every couple of minutes as the cage rolled on. Soon, the cage slowed and grew dark until Cólion couldn't see anything. For a few moments Cólion only saw darkness, then it suddenly got lighter. But it was still dim and hot.

Soon, Cólion's forehead was dripping with sweat from the uncomfortable heat.

Cólion realised he was in the heart of the drac's home.

He glanced around at the makeshift homes that the drac's had built. The wooden homes looked old, the wood seemed almost bloated because of the intense heat. The stone ground was crumbled and full of rubble where the drac's had often travelled. Beyond the houses, Cólion could see a sickly green fog that seemed to hover over the filthy water.

Cólion felt a clawed hand reach through the bars and grab his brown hair, brutally slamming him into the iron bars. He gasped, tasting coppery blood in his mouth as the drac leaned in close. Cólion opened his eyes, staring in fear at the drac's twisted features.

His face looked like wrinkled bark and his teeth ranged from yellow to black. His ears were shredded and he stank of alcohol. His skin was burnt and crusty from the intense heat, a nasty yellowed brown that made Cólion flinch.

The drac grinned. His features crinkling even more as he gave Cólion a sickening smile.

'This will be your new home, you pathetic welp.' His smile disappeared. He used his other hand and pulled out a curved dagger, pointing the tip at Cólion's cheek.

'First things first.' He sneered.

Cólion's breath hitched and he closed his eyes as the blade neared his face. He heard a gasp, then a snarl and the drac released him. Cólion scrambled backwards and looked through the bars.

A man with dark ginger hair was facing the drac, crouching in a defensive position. The drac's knife in hand, he waited for the drac to strike.

'It's my prisoner, mutt!' The drac hissed.

'Prisoner or not, that elf is already beaten and a captive.' He replied calmly. 'There is no need to make it worse.'

The drac roared in fury, charging the man head on, pulling another pair of knives from his belt. The man waited until the drac was inches away before he swept the drac's legs out from under him. The drac landed heavily on his stomach before the man pinned him down.

'Enough. Do I need to embarrass you further?' The man said. 'There is no point in hurting a defenseless enemy.'

The drac grunted and the man let him up, handing the blade back. The man walked over to Cólion's cage, his wild hair sticking out from every angle. His deep tan skin looked almost orange in the sickly light.

Cólion pressed himself as far back as he could as the stranger got closer.

Cólion looked at the man for the first time. A pair of green-hazel eyes stared back. A knot of dread forming in his stomach.

This man was clearly a maikong.

The maikong stopped in front of the cage and bent over to undo the lock before reaching in and firmly pulling Cólion out by the arm. He held Cólion for a second before turning him over. Cólion felt the bonds on his ankles snap.

The maikong gently set Cólion on his feet before he smiled broadly. His wide smile reaching the corners of his twinkling eyes.

'Sorry about all this,' the maikong said sadly. 'The drac's take prisoners and it's our job to take care of them until something changes. My name is Cedar.'

Cólion glared up at him. He couldn't be serious.

'I'm Cólion,' he grumbled.

Cedar cocked his head. 'Does that mean something in your language?'

'It means gold.' Cólion huffed.

'Ah. I see,' Cedar said as he ruffled Cólion's hair. 'Your name means gold because of your hair!'

Finding Your Way

by Tarana Begum

Siara was lying down on the nest enjoying the morning sun. Her body was absorbing the heat and warming her dearly, while her grey skin glistened against the light. She was radiating. Her large yellow eyes closed just so she could feel the heat and serene surroundings. As she was relaxing, she felt her pointed elf ears that stuck outwards, twitching. She could feel something was picking at her grey horns on her head. As she opened her eyes, she saw a small, orange-red dragon looking down at her. She smiled up at the dragon.

'Hello Torchi, what are you doing?' Torchi smiled at her with his short but spiky tail playfully swaying from side to side.

'Siara, you said you would play with us today,' Siara laughed hearing this.

'Of course I will but first let me go on over to Delgar,' she said getting up.

'Aw do you really have to go?' Torchi said feeling a little sad, 'can't you just skip it?' he asked eagerly, as his red wings flapped.

'You know I can't do that, I like talking to him,' Torchi sighed.

'Yes I know but be quick. Today we're playing Flying Phantom - I'm the Phantom!' He said excitedly while his small ears flapped.

'Ok I will,' Siara laughed. Once she stood, she stretched her tall slender body, her elf ears twitched and she headed towards the large brown stoned hut that Delgar resided in.

'Delgar it's me,' Siara announced as she entered into the grounds.

'Ah, Siara, please come in,' Delgar said in his deep voice. Delgar was the strongest and eldest dragon, or better known as the Elder Dragon. His scaly skin drowned in the colour of blood red from his head to the tip of his tail. His spine formed ripples of wrinkles that showed his age but he was not to be taken lightly. His long, sharp teeth were able to cause harm that could devour an entire race. Not to mention his large golden yellow eyes that pierced through anyone with just a sharp look. He was very intimidating and was the

Elder Dragon for a reason; he was a powerful and wise creature.

When Siara entered the room she saw Delgar on his throne reading a book while his smooth but wrinkled belly was exposed, he looked relaxed. Had it been anyone else, they would have been terrified at this sight but not Siara.

'I've just come to say hello,' she said with a smile. Delgar looked down at the tiny creature before him. He stretched out his short arm with his dagger-like claws spread open and bent down to reach for Siara. Siara crawled onto his palm which he lifted and moved towards his shoulder. She sat there comfortably as Delgar started to read his book again.

'You know, you're the only one that makes me look weak,' Delgar said staring at the pages of his book, 'the dragons fear me and yet you are the only one I don't seem to have that effect on.'

'Well it's your own fault,' Siara smiled swaying her long legs back and forth.

'How so?' Delgar asked curiously while looking to the side of his shoulder to stare at Siara. His hope was that this would intimidate her but it failed.

'Well,' she said tilting her head towards one side. 'You treated me like one of your own even though I'm not and I was raised here so of course you looked out for me from the start. Everyone knows how you feel and no one dares to question,' Delgar smiled with his long monstrous looking teeth in full view, 'of course, no one will ever think you're weak with those teeth that look like claws,'

'Hey!' Delgar yelled deeply, Siara laughed. Just then, Siara heard Torchi's voice from outside yelling.

'Fly! Or be mine!' He let out an evil laugh. He blew out flames from his mouth as he flew around chasing the other dragons.

'Torchi! How many times do I have to tell you? No flame breathing when playing!' Torchi's mother flew to where he was in the sky and grabbed him, with her claws, by his spikey coral tail and started dragging him down.

'Ow! Mum, don't hurt me. Please let me go, I won't do it anymore!' Torchi whined.

'Oh no, I need to punish you. Stay indoors and no flying,' Torchi's mother responded.

'Noo!' Torchi whined while being dragged back down. Siara looked at them, saddened.

'What's the matter?' Delgar enquired, placing the book aside.

'I've been thinking for a while, I want to know about my family. I want to go travelling to find out about them.' Delgar paused for a moment looking at Siara and then reverted to his book.

'Are you sure you want to? I thought we were your family?' He said quietly.

'Oh, of course you are Delgar,' Siara hugged the side of his neck, 'but I want to know about my family, I'm clearly not a dragon but I wish I was. I just want to know more about my parents.' Delgar did not say a word; he did not want to protest. It was not right, she was old enough to do what she liked and had the right to know the whereabouts of her parents.

'Very well,' he voiced approvingly. He placed her on the ground gently, shifted to get off the throne on all fours and stood up on his legs. He shrunk himself from a giant to that of a regular sized dragon, which was as tall as a mountain. 'I guess we should go over the basics before you leave shall we?' Siara nodded eagerly waiting to learn, 'I'll have to tell you about the world and the different places and races so let's begin.' Delgar cleared his throat and then with a point of his claw began to draw out the map of the world. Wisps of lights started to appear as he did. The lights were drawing out the shapes of the map as Delgar began to explain, 'The world that we live in has eight main places that are very important. Let us start with Fogvalor, a stone city. It was created by drac's as a mutual ground for all races. There is also a red and blue flame to represent both species of elf. There are even underground burrows and passages to many places in the city for gnomes. Then there is Waque, built high up in the mountains, home to the elves. Near Waque is Drakland, home to drac's. Ceat is place for magic users and magical creatures to go and train. They are the only ones who are able to enter; dragons and magic users are the only creatures to enter. Next to Ceat is Kai Darl, an ancient underground city and home to the gnomes' race only. Tuskbane city is parted into three districts known as Farming and Agriculture, Artisanal and Market and lastly the Governmental District. This city is home of the lepus race. The home of the maikong is The High Wilds. Lastly, we have Lastra, the floating city. This is where we live. As you can see, there is no specific place on the map because it's constantly moving.'

Each time Delgar described a place, the wispy lights illustrated another section of the map until it was completed. Lastra and Ceat were the only two that were not joined. Siara nodded and understood this completely, she was smart and a quick study after all. She thought to herself that Delgar really was the wise Elder Dragon.

'And that's why I keep seeing different surroundings,' Siara thought.

'Exactly. In fact many species are not aware that this place exists.' Delgar said. 'Now, when it comes to the races, you must be very careful because there are so many.' He paused for a moment. He had a tiny drop of blue light on the tip of his claw, which he flicked at the illuminated drawing of the map. Instantly, the map glowed a blinding bright blue light with shimmers all around and turned into paper. He handed it over to Siara, 'here take this with you, you're going to need it.' Siara took the map and nodded, fascinated by the magic wielded by Delgar. 'Now, as for the races, I have written down what you need to know. Take this to read and anything you don't understand ask me.' He instructed.

Siara looked at the different races, she began reading aloud, starting with the elf race.

'The elf race are not immortal beings. They can get hurt and are of different shapes and sizes, with grey skin. Dracs are a race that have horns in a variety of sizes, pointed tails and red eyes. They are a darker elf but they are not all demonic creatures in their nature. Gnomes are a shorter race. Dragons are very smelly creatures,' Siara hid a smile as she watched Delgar's reaction; he was pacing back and forth and came to a halt.

'Hey! It doesn't say that,' he eyed Siara. She laughed.

'No of course it doesn't say that, I just wanted to tease you,' Siara responded. Delgar sighed a puff of smoke. Siara continued to read, 'dragons are thought to be extinct but there may be one or two hidden around as well as eggs that may be scattered.' Siara paused, she looked up at Delgar, 'What do you mean one or two dragons? There are so many here.' She pointed around her.

'This text about the race is not quite accurate. In fact, what you see in Lastra is probably all there is. We are creatures of magic and because of that, witches tend to feel threatened. Especially because their magic does not affect us.' Delgar explained. Siara slowly nodded, understanding.

'So witches use dark magic?' She asked as Delgar nodded.

'That's correct,' Siara looked back at the races and saw that there were two races left, the lepus, a humanoid-bunny and maikong, a humanoid-fox.

After reading about the races, Siara fell quiet, 'What about me? What kind of race am I?' She asked.

'You're a hybrid of an elf and drac, known as an elfrac,' Delgar explained.

'Is that why I have grey skin like an elf and horns like a drac?' The Elder Dragon nodded. Siara's heart started to beat after learning more about herself.

'You must be careful though; many are not familiar with a creature like you and can easily mistake you for a demonic drac,' Delgar warned her. Siara nodded, showing that she understood.

'Don't worry, I'll be careful.' She beamed at him.

Just then, Torchi flew in and tumbled into Siara, whose pointed tail tangled up with his.

'Siara! Are you ready to play yet?' He said excitedly,

'Oh, silly Torchi, you didn't have to fall onto me,' Siara laughed.

'I know but I was excited and-' Torchi froze; he looked up at Delgar, who was watching intently at them. 'Oh my God! Your Highness…I mean Sir Majesty I mean…' Torchi started to stumble.

'Oh don't worry Torchi,' Delgar said looking rather amused about the situation. 'Siara is all yours, she's been telling me how much she wants to play with you.' The tension in Torchi was released. He was feeling a little more relaxed and excited to play with Siara.

'Come on Torchi, let's go play Flying Phantom. This time, I'll be the phantom,' Torchi gleamed and excitedly zoomed out of the hut with eagerness.

Siara looked up at Delgar, 'thank you Delgar, I really appreciate everything you've done for me.' Delgar gave a slight nod and Siara went out to play.

After a lot of fun flying with Torchi and the others, that night Siara could not sleep. She was feeling sad that she was going to leave. She was excited to learn about her parents and finding out where they are but on the other hand she was going to miss Lastra. After all, this was her home and a place where she spent all of her time with the nearly extinct species that live in secret, not discovered by others. The city was hidden, kept out of prying eyes by a protection spell casted by Delgar, so no one can find it. Siara made a promise to Delgar to never reveal this place or the existence of dragons, as they feared that it would disrupt their peace and cause harm to others.

The next day, Siara said goodbye to Torchi, he was hugging her so tightly. 'I'll be back Torchi, don't worry. I'm not going forever,' Siara told him. Torchi was not happy with this but still let her go.

'I'm going to miss you so much,' he sadly cried.

'Me too,' Siara said feeling glum.

'Now Siara, remember the promise,' Delgar said and she nodded, 'you know you're an elfrac so there will be others that may attack you because they have never seen a creature like you. Maybe you should wear a cloak to hide your horns.'

'No,' Siara shook her head, 'I don't want to hide my race just because I'm a little different. If I did that, people would think I'm really hiding something and must be evil.'

Delgar nodded in understanding and then paused for a moment, 'the only thing I know about your parents is that your mother is an elf named Sillia and your father is a drac.'

Siara thought about her mother, wondering what she might look like. Delgar then gave her a necklace with a rare pink crystal, 'Take this necklace. It will help you to find Lastra and is also a way for you to communicate with dragons. The only other way to communicate with a dragon is by another dragon or their blood, so don't lose this.' Siara took the necklace, carefully placing it around her neck.

'Thank you,' she said.

'Ok, let us go.' Delgar said. He was still in his downsized form as he placed Siara on his back. There was a small, blood red piercing horn on Delgar's back. Siara held to it tightly as he flapped out his dark red wings and began to fly away from Lastra city and down to the lands.

Delgar dropped her on the bottom left corner near Fogvalor, in an empty forest. He flew away giving Siara a hug, telling her she can contact him anytime. Siara looked at the map and saw that she needed to head north to the centre of Fogvalor, where the markets and most of the creatures reside.

When she finally arrived near the end of the forest,

she heard whimpering coming from the east side. She followed the sound to find an injured maikong on the ground holding onto his wound. She noticed a drac coming closer to the maikong ready to attack again. Just then, Siara formed her pointed fingers together that had moulded a small circle immersed with blue and white energy and threw it at the drac which injured it. The drac looked at Siara, his whole body was ready to attack but he halted; instead, he glared at her and then ran off. Siara ran to the maikong to help with his injuries.

'Hey, are you ok? What's your name?' She asked him feeling concerned.

'It's Ming, I'm fine, just-' Ming looked at Siara and suddenly a surge of fear instilled within him. 'Stay away from me!' He yelled terrified of Siara, 'You're a drac!' and ran off limping before Siara could even explain herself. Siara was saddened but refused to dwell on it too much. Delgar did warn her not to push someone to try and understand as it can lead to more misunderstandings.

Just as she approached near the centre of Fogvalor, she heard a scream and instinctively followed it to find what looked to be two short lepus's. One was injured and the other looked concerned while huddled over. Siara rushed immediately to help, not caring about the consequences of them also rejecting her help.

'Elpina stop worrying, I'll be fine,' said the injured lepus.

'Elpin no! Stop talking you're too hurt,' said Elpina feeling very worried.

'What happened?' Siara asked kneeling down to help. Elpina was stunned by the creature in front of her but snapped out of it the moment Siara spoke.

'He's really hurt. He was dancing to my singing and then tripped and hurt himself on a spike,' Elpina pointed to the spear looking weapon. Siara looked at the wound on Elpin's upper arm.

'It's a deep cut,' she told herself. It wasn't a problem for her, she immediately placed her long, slender pointed fingers over the injury and out came a blue glow. The wounded area completely healed. Elpin was stunned by this miraculous work; he looked up at Siara and gawped at the beauty. 'Are you ok?' She asked feeling concerned.

Elpin snapped out of his daze and instead was filled with so much energy that he jumped back up on his two bunny looking feet and said, 'I'm fine.' He began dancing happily again, Siara laughed while Elpina glared at him feeling concerned about his health, 'I'm fine Elpina.' He said as he held her hands and danced. Elpina then looked at Siara and asked her curiously.

'Who are you?'

'Oh I'm Siara. I'm looking for my mother, she is an

elf named Sillia,' Siara responded.

'Where are you from?' Elpina asked. Siara took a short pause, remembering her promise to Delgar.

'I can't remember, I've sort of lost my memories,' she felt a little bad about lying but she had to.

'What are you? I've never seen an elf look like you,' Elpin asked, curious about this beautiful creature.

'I'm an elfrac,' Siara felt hesitant as she said this because she didn't know how they would react.

'What's that?' Both Elpin and Elpina asked in unison, so Siara explained it to them. 'You know many will fear you, because you look like a drac even though you're half elf. You should be careful.' Elpina voiced.

'I will, don't worry,'

'Now you won't have to!' Elpin responded, 'We want to join you in your adventure. After all, you did just save my life and I think it would be fun.' Elpina nodded enthusiastically agreeing.

'That's great! I would love some company,' she said, 'So what's your story?'

'Well I'm Elpin; I'm from Tuskbane City, from the Artisanal and Market district. Unfortunately, because of the flood, I lost my family and home. I was alone for most of my life,' Elpin said smiling sadly.

'I'm Elpina,' Elpina said, trying to distract Elpin from feeling sad. 'I'm from Tuskbane city as well but the Farming and Agriculture district. I met Elpin while

I was farming near the streams and he came through it. I was farming food for the lepus's at the Artisanal and Market district. We ended up becoming best friends and we both wanted to explore the world. That was many years ago. Since then, we've been travelling to many places.'

'It's fun exploring!' Elpin said happily.

Siara and the others ended up going to the market in Fogvalor to see if anyone had heard of Sillia and her whereabouts. They noticed how others were looking at Siara cautiously and fearfully. Some pointed and whispered but Siara ignored them, as she was determined to find her mother. Elpin, on the other hand, decided to cut the tension. He ended up taking Siara by the hands and started dancing and singing, showing to others that she was harmless. Siara laughed and Elpina decided to sing. Slowly, they noticed the crowds around them loosening up; though there were still some who were weary. Siara approached a passer-by, an elf.

'Have you heard of someone called Sillia? I'm looking for her,' she asked, the elf shook her head and walked on,

'Sillia did you say?' Another passer-by said, 'I've heard of the name,' it was another elf.

'You have?' Siara asked excitedly, 'What's your

name?'

'Yes, I have and my name is Miole. You are?' Miole asked, amazed at her beauty. 'I'm Siara. Have you seen her?'

'No,' Miole shook his head, 'I haven't seen her but I have heard of the name being mentioned by a guard at the border between Fogvalor and Waque.'

'Oh that's wonderful! Can you please direct me to where the border is?' She asked him kindly, Miole grinned,

'I'll do one better, I'll take you there myself. I have some business at Waque anyway.'

At the border, there were two short elves on guard; they both had spikes and a metal shield.

'You once mentioned the name Sillia correct?' Miole asked the elf on the left.

'Yes but it was just a legendary story that I heard that took place many years ago, I don't know the full story.'

'Do you know who might know?' Miole asked.

'Rio might know,' the elf on the right answered, 'he knows a lot about the elf history. You can find him in Green Slugs and Jelly's.'

'Thank you,' Siara responded.

'I can't join but I'll show you which way to go,' Miole said, 'I have some business to take care of.' Siara nodded.

'Thank you,' she headed to find Rio with Elpin and Elpina. Miole left them knowing they would be fine and then walked the other direction. As they strolled through Waque, they saw all kinds of elves. There was an elf stealing food from one of the market stalls, while another helped an elf that fell. There was also a tall elf who was holding a protest of some kind, gathered with many different elves who surrounded him. They noticed that Waque also had a light red fog in the air that was strange.

Once they arrived at Green Slugs and Jelly's, they noticed the lively atmosphere even inside the shop. The place was diverse of elves ranging from all shapes and sizes. From the far left side of the shop, a fight broke out from two elves; one was short while the other was tall. Then there was a huge crowd in the centre that was hard to miss with one elf in the middle playing cards on the big round dark wooden table. He seemed to be winning a lot of gold while clearly cheating as he had two cards on the side of his pocket.

'Nice one Rio,' one of the elves said praising Rio.

'I guess we found Rio,' Elpina said reluctantly. Siara nodded and once Rio finished his game, she approached him.

'My, my, what do we have here?' Rio asked, he knelt

back on his chair. The crowd around them fell quiet. Rio was a short elf, with a big belly and had pointed ears that were a little large on his head.

'Hello Rio, I am Siara. I'll get straight to the point. Please tell me what you know about an elf named Sillia.' There was a glint in Rio's small green eyes.

'Oh no, you can't just get that information for free,' Rio greedily demanded.

'Ok,' Siara nodded not worried about this and handed over 2,000 gold. Rio looked at it unsatisfied.

'Oh no, this isn't going to be enough, I need 50,000 gold.' The crowd around him started to smirk and giggle. Siara could easily afford this but she did not want to flaunt her wealth, as it would raise the suspicion of others.

'I don't have that much gold,' she said.

'Well then no information but thanks for the gold.' He grabbed the gold, cackled and ran away. Siara felt dejected not knowing how else to get the information.

'I know how you can get that much gold,' Elpina said wanting to cheer Siara up. 'Gnomes usually can give you gold or get you some. There are some gnomes at Fogvalor that may be able to help but of course we have to wait till dark. The city never sleeps as gnomes are able to come out and play and do business at night, otherwise known as the Night Sweeper.'

'That's great. We'll ask the gnomes,' Siara said.

Elpina made a face thinking it may not be such a good idea.

'I don't know if you would think so. You see, gnomes usually ask for something in return and it's almost always a high price.'

'It's better for me to know what that price is then do nothing,' Siara said feeling headstrong.

'Good thing it will become nightfall by the time we arrive in Fogvalor,' Elpin said jumping excitedly.

As soon as they left Waque and arrived at the mountain forest, it illuminated with a blue flame. However, the Zisu - a type of white bird - were nowhere around.

'I don't like the look of this,' Siara said feeling uneasy while observing her surroundings. Slowly emerging out of the woods and mountains were multiple elves, sneering. At first, they each came one at a time, suddenly, a herd of them came at once pushing and shoving and cutting Siara and the lepus's. Each cut started to make Siara's blood boil a little until finally she gave in to her drac's blood. Her previously yellow eyes were now glowing red, her horns rooted out even more and her aura completely changed. There was steam coming out of the wounds as they started to heal. The elves stopped and started to back away feeling fearful. She pointed her long finger at one of the elves and in a blink of an eye made a cut on every elf present.

'What's going on?' One of them panicked. Every cut was deep and weakened them. Until finally they were unable to move. Siara's blood was rushing from the joy, she smirked at the wounded creatures and the urge to kill became strong.

'Siara! Stop!' Both Elpin and Elpina yelled in unison. They feared that she may have actually killed them. Siara snapped out of it, her eyes turned yellow again. The elves who were conscious took this chance to escape. Both the lepus' looked at each other with concern for Siara, wondering what that was. Siara remained silent, as she was not sure how to explain what had just happened.

After the quiet journey back to Fogvalor, it was completely dark; the place really did look like another city. It was bustling even more than before, with the additional race of gnomes. The stone walls that made this city were illuminating brightly. The place was lively as you felt you were being swept away in the night. Night Sweeper was very fitting. They approached a gnome merchant that looked like she was selling some priceless décor pieces. Luckily, there was not a crowd around the table as Siara approached.

'What can I do for you young elf?' the gnome asked her, without concern for Siara's appearance.

'Hi I'm Siara, I need help. How can I get more

gold?' She asked.

'I'm Cliandra. I can get you some gold in exchange for a favour,' she smiled kindly at Siara.

'What is it?' She asked ready for anything.

'I need you to get me a rare plant called Cogolish,' she grinned. 'It's located in The High Wilds, so I'd be careful.'

As they rested from walking, Elpina looked worried.

'Siara I don't think we can enter there. Maikong's live there and they don't allow any other race to enter.'

'I have to try no matter what,' Siara said determined.

The next morning, they headed to The High Wilds. Once they arrived at the border, Siara and the others noticed how the two maikong guards, tall in their fox-like manner, stood there while sleeping. They were practically drooling. Elpin became excited.

'Yes! We can enter!' He said running past the guards.

'No! Elpin come back!' Siara whispered as loud as she could. Just then, a large maikong jumped out viciously standing on all fours, growling at Elpin. Elpin screamed at the top of his lungs and ran fast behind Siara. The maikong glared and sneered at Siara, fully ready to attack.

'I don't want any harm,' Siara said calmly, 'I just need some help.'

'Leave!' The maikong growled.

'Please-'

'I said leave!' He growled again.

'Wait, Koga,' came a familiar cry from inside the border, 'she is the one that saved me from that drac.'

'Ming, so she was the one.' Koga looked at Siara. 'Very well you may come in but not the lepus's,' he glared at Elpin.

'They will come in with me, they mean no harm,' Siara said in a firm and strong tone,

'Very well.' Koga said feeling slightly fearful from the way Siara spoke.

They entered through the gate and crossed over a bridge to get to the other side of the river. 'You may follow me, they can stay here,' Koga instructed. He reverted to standing on two legs, he was clearly an Alpha. Siara looked concerned for her friends that were surrounded by the cautious looking maikongs. 'Don't worry. They will not attack unless I give the command,' He shook his head at the pack and they all loosened. Once they were alone, Koga asked suspiciously, 'What are you?'

'I'm an elfrac,' She replied,

'Ah, I see. I am sorry for nearly attacking you; I thought you were a drac from Drakland. Since there was a war many years ago with them, we managed to live out our time here without mixing with other races. It's purely a safety precaution. Of course, maikongs do come and go here but we rarely allow any other race to enter. You must be careful, as some may actually attack you thinking you may be a drac.'

'I will be cautious,' Siara replied. This was starting to feel a bit like Déjà vu. Siara understood why they were such a cautious species and why Ming had reacted the way he did when he saw her.

'Ming has gone to get the plant. I would be happy if you took him with you on your travels. I feel you might get hurt,' Koga said.

'No that is fine.'

'No, I insist, you did save him.' Koga replied, just then Ming entered. 'Ah, here he is now. Ming I would like you to accompany Siara on her journey.' At hearing this, Ming started to feel angry. He was not a people person after all and preferred it that way.

'Absolutely not,' he refused.

'Ming!' Koga's tone changed to that of a leader, 'that's an order.'

'Yes sir,' Ming mumbled, not happy.

As they travelled back to Fogvalor, Ming was very quiet and still feeling grumpy for having to join a drac. Siara, on the other hand, knew she would either be liked or disliked but didn't say much. Instead, she was playing with Elpin up ahead.

'You know she's actually a very kind soul. She's nothing like those dracs we know,' Elpina said trying to understand Ming's cautiousness. However, Ming didn't say a word but observed her carefully.

'Here you go,' Siara said handing over the Cogolish plant to Cliandra.

'Thank you. It will take me two days to get you your gold. I'll be mining for it in Kai Darl,' Siara nodded.

As they waited for the gold, they started to explore Fogvalor. When they started to get a little hungry, Siara asked, 'so what food should we get?'

'Hmm…' Elpin said thoughtfully thinking about food, 'Colballs sounds good.'

'Isn't that meat from a bird?' Ming asked feeling a little hungry himself, Elpin nodded.

'If we're all good with Colballs, I can get some from that stall over there,' Elpina said pointing at a stall where there were different kinds of Colballs being served. Everyone nodded in agreement and Elpina went off to buy the food. While they waited, Siara glanced over at Ming feeling concerned.

'How are you?' She asked him. Ming was eyeing Siara suspiciously.

'Why do you ask?' He asked thinking that the drac

must really be up to something.

'Well you got hurt after all and I wasn't able to offer you any help when I first saw you.' Her eyes went over to his now bandaged wound. Ming felt a little embarrassed now for thinking she had bad intentions. She was trying to help him and he just misjudged her and ran.

'It's not so bad. That Cogolish plant is an herb that heals deep wounds, though it takes a while but I'm doing fine.'

'Do you mind if I have a look?' Siara asked. Ming looked at her hesitantly.

'You should let her look at your wounds,' Elpin suddenly popped out staring down at the wound. 'She healed my arm and now I feel incredible!' He said excitedly while dancing around. Siara laughed.

'You don't have to listen you him,' Siara said trying to be cautious of how Ming was feeling.

'You healed his wound?' Ming said shocked by this. 'What are you?' he asked feeling a little fearful.

'I'm an elfrac, part drac and part elf.' She explained about her parents and this time Ming was softer on her and allowed her to heal him. He felt every part of his pain disappear. Ming felt that he could let his guard down a little in front of Siara now. Just then, Elpina arrived with the food as they spent their next couple of days eating, talking and resting. During this time,

Siara felt that she could trust her new companions and decided to tell them the truth about not losing her memories. She told them exactly where she was from. However, none of them truly believed it although they have never seen an elfrac before, so they decided that she must be telling them the truth.

Two days later, Cliandra arrived with the gold and they headed back to Waque, where they found Rio messing around as usual. They handed the gold over to him.

'Nice work,' Rio responded smirking. 'From what I know, Sillia was actually a Witch and she cast a spell on a drac to make him fall in love with her-'

Siara's blood started to boil at the lies being spewed. Her eyes turned red her whole body was letting out an evil aura. She pointed at the elf and sent him flying across the room. The room fell quiet from what they just witnessed. Rio was injured all over and could barely move, even though he sensed this elf was powerful and he sent out those mischievous elves to attack, he was stunned by such power. Siara smirked at the weakling before her.

'I can hear your blood boiling, enjoying the lies you spewed,' Siara voiced sternly with a deep echo.

'All I know is that Sillia was killed by an evil creature and was buried in Drakland,' Rio panicked.

'What? Killed?' Siara returned to her normal state,

her eyes turned yellow as she simmered down with a little wisp of white smoke surrounding her. Once she was completely calm, she discovered that her next journey was to Drakland. Her heart was beating really fast as the words still echoed in her head. She couldn't believe that her mother was dead. All she ever thought was that her mother was missing and that was why she was never around her. Once she found her, she wanted to ask about her drac father. No one would abandon their child, she had completely convinced herself of that. She would have left Lastra a lot sooner to go and look for her but she had felt that she wasn't ready and was very naïve of the world. She knew elfrac's were a rare species; there was so little information on them that no one truly knew how powerful they were. Even Delgar himself had told her that he was not familiar with it.

Siara was not convinced that her mother was in fact dead. She was determined to find out all the information she could. Elpin, Elpina and Ming all saw what she did and felt fear for her power. They had no idea what she was capable of and they didn't think that Siara was sure either. Just as they left the restaurant, Miole was outside, shocked to his core at the power he just witnessed. He managed to compose himself before Siara noticed.

'Miole? What are you doing here?' Siara asked surprised by the elf.

'I heard the ruckus and the next thing I hear is that you find out your mother is…' he trailed off. Siara felt a pang of sting in her heart.

'It can't be true,' she said, in denial of the whole thing. 'My mother is just missing. I just need to find her, in Drakland.'

Miole did not want to leave her in such a state, no matter how much she seems to look fine, he knew that she was hiding it.

'I have nothing to do right now, mind if I join you?' he asked her with the intention of wanting to keep her safe. Siara looked at Miole knowing that he was probably worried about her.

'That's fine,' she said monotonously. She tried so hard to smile at how caring and thoughtful he was being to her but she couldn't. Her mind was full of thoughts about her mother in Drakland.

Later that day, Rio was at Drakland half beaten and limping. He entered the Kark Palace where there was a guard near the entryway.

'I need to speak to Drakol,' Rio voiced angrily, breathing heavily and holding onto his wound.

'I can't let you in,' the elf guard said. Rio felt his blood boil with rage as nothing was going his way. He lost his patience completely as he grabbed the small guard by the throat and started to punch the guard in the stomach. This made him feel a little better, as he got it out of his system. Nearly beaten to death, the guard was left on the floor, unconscious, while Rio entered the palace casually. Once he entered, he found himself in the spacious hall. Rio paused feeling a surge of pain which he thought was his wounds but then he noticed his grey skin changing in colour.

'Argh!' He screamed in pain until finally it stopped, he looked at his body. His wounds were completely healed and there was this new surge of power residing in him. Grinning at the new change, Rio felt his blood boil with indignation.

When he entered the grand hall, he saw Drakol on his throne, who looked up.

'Ah Rio, I almost didn't recognise you. I see you've become a drac.' Drakol grinned feeling proud, 'well done.'

'Thank you, your Majesty, anything to be of use,' he smirked and Drakol laughed.

'I can hear your blood boiling through the lie; you must be really enjoying this,' Rio smiled. His true intention was to get as much gold as he could get his hands on and with his new found strength, it was just as easy.

'Of course. I am more capable in this state,' he said. Drakol looked at him smiling.

'So who did you end up killing? As that's the only way someone could become an evil drac,' Drakol asked.

'Just some lowly guard but I didn't kill him, though he's on the brink of death.'

'Make sure to clean up his body well,' Drakol ordered some of the other dracs in the room.

'Yes Sir,' many of them said in unison and disappeared.

Drakol looked at Rio 'well I assume you've actually come here with some news?' he asked curiously.

'Yes your Majesty,' Rio said kneeling down, 'an elf named Siara was asking about Sillia.'

'Oh?' Drakol said intrigued.

'But there's something different about this elf. She looks like an elf but had red eyes and her power is incredible.'

'That's interesting,' Drakol said, wanting to meet this new found power that seemed to have made even Rio feel fear. The only time Rio ever looked this scared was when he was in front of Drakol. The look of mercilessly killing and the bloodlust in his eyes had him powerless and unable to move. Drakol was definitely curious about this elf who he wanted to encounter himself. He was feeling bored as there were no strong opponents around. 'Have the dracs not attack her. I want to see this Siara for myself. If anyone else gets in the way... kill them.' He demanded with a sneer, as his black skin started to shimmer, with his grey scar on his forehead clearly visible. 'Tolga you know what to do,' the drac standing next to Drakol nodded and vanished.

Siara and the others silently travelled towards Drakland, Miole looked at Siara who looked to be deep in thought.

'Are you ok?' He asked her, Siara just nodded. She didn't want to talk, all she wanted was answers. Her mind was filled with thoughts about her mother, she was not dead, she thought to herself repeatedly. The rest looked at her and felt saddened. Ming was also feeling a little upset about it, he could only imagine what she must be thinking. He never experienced anything like that himself, he was always with his family, his pack. They knew where he was and he knew where they were too. To not be able to know about one's own family must be a lonely life, he thought to himself. Both Elpin and Elpina felt a pang of loss from their own family but to have them murdered is beyond reason. They both knew Siara a little more than the rest and they knew she was a considerate and cheerful elf. Seeing her the way she was now was making them feel uneasy and hurt. All they ever want to do is try to protect her, find the answers and help her in any way possible.

When they finally arrived in Drakland, Siara noticed the intensity of the red fog compared to how it was in Waque. It was definitely something strange and she didn't know what the cause was. They were near some wooden buildings and noticed the stream of water, which looked almost black. There were many clouds of red fog that puffed out and polluted the area. The streets were stained red as well. Siara looked around the place, feeling uneasy she noticed something as well.

'I don't like this,' she said concerned about her surroundings. Miole was also very cautious.

'I agree. This place is usually a lot more unfriendly in their form of greeting.'

'No one is attacking us, just a lot of red eyes glaring at us,' Siara said, looking at the many unfriendly auras around them. Miole told Siara how this place is ruled over by an evil king known as Drakol. If anyone would know answers to Siara's questions, it would be him. 'Someone must have told them we were coming,' Siara thought that it must have been Rio as he was the only one who would have ties around these areas and with their king. Just at that moment, Siara sensed someone was behind her. As she abruptly turned, she saw someone there covered in a cloak.

'His Majesty will see you now,' he voiced calmly. Everyone looked at the guy, curious and highly suspicious of him but they followed. Miole felt a strange feeling of familiarity towards this guy but didn't exactly know why and thought to himself that he must have been mistaken.

Once they arrived at Krark Palace, they noticed how the place seemed to have been swarming with dracs. Instantly, one after another they came after them, except for Siara. Siara was just about to hit them with a spark when a group of dracs jumped in front of her crumbling the ground with their strength. Siara was separated from her group instantly.

'Elpin! Elpina! Ming! Miole!' She yelled making sure they were ok.

'We're fine!' Miole yelled back, drawing out a sword which he then used to slash some of the dracs, 'go on ahead! We can handle this!'

'But I can't just leave you guys here!' Siara felt concerned.

'We're fine! Just go!' Ming yelled. Siara knew that she was not going to be of help here. The only way to stop a crowd of dracs like this was to find the source and stop him first.

'I'm going,' she said with determination, 'I'm leaving it up to you all!' She said and she ran towards the throne room.

Miole felt the wind of a sword flying towards him which he stopped just in time. It was the guy in the cloak, his hood had fallen off, exposing his face. He was a drac but he looked like someone that Miole knew. 'Tolga…' he said in shock, 'is that you? You're alive? I can't believe this! It's me, Miole.' Tolga's cold eyes looked at Miole.

'I have no idea who you are,' and slashed his right arm. Miole held onto his injured arm.

'Tolga how can you forget? It's me-' he then noticed how his childhood friend, the elf, has now become an evil drac. 'No way.' Miole fell into shock still clutching at his arm bleeding. 'What happened to you?' Tolga came dashing towards him, with his sword, ready to kill Miole, who just stood there still in shock of seeing his friend. Tolga was just about to hit his target when he felt two paws holding his legs and before he could turn to see who it was, he was dragged off the ground and swung against the wall.

'Get a hold of yourself!' Ming said. Miole snapped out of his shock and started to attack the other dracs.

Siara finally arrived in the throne room, where she saw this dark figure sitting on the throne. The unbelievable power emitting from him was so incredible that Siara was stricken with fear. She took very slow but heavy steps towards Drakol.

'Oh my, what an interesting creature you are,' Drakol said with a bloodlust dripping from every word. 'What are you exactly? You are clearly not an elf,' he asked smiling as Siara stood by the steps of the throne.

'Where is Sillia?' she voiced sternly, determined to get answers. Drakol laughed, feeling highly amused by her display of bravery.

'My, what bravery you have to speak to me like that,' he said. 'I'll do the honour of asking you again, what are you?'

As soon as Drakol finished speaking, he noticed a cut on his cheek which started to bleed a little. He looked up at Siara who was standing there, with her pointed fingers in the shape of a flick and ready to flick again. Drakol let out a sigh.

'Okay. Now I'm mad,' he said as he exerts one of his fingers to let out a small blue energy ball which speeds towards Siara. She dodged the ball which ended up hitting a pillar in the room, crumbling it to the ground. As she dodged the ball, Siara appeared in a flash next to Drakol, about to hit him when he dodged it, landing Siara's fist on this throne chair turning it into dust.

'That was my favourite chair,' Drakol complained. Even though he was playing around, he knew had that made contact, he would have lost his head. Siara did not leave anytime to mess around as she went after him again in a flash of speed. This time, Drakol had to use more strength than usual to block his face. He pushed her using his strength and she went flying across the room, smashing into the wall. 'I'm getting tired of this,' he said as he blasted another energy ball. Siara was mostly able to dodge so that the energy ball only hit her left arm.

Drakol hit her with another energy ball and this time made impact, sending Siara through multiple pillars in the room until she smashed against the wall. This time, she was unable to move. 'I must admit that you are exactly like Tolga said you are. Strong and fast as well. It was definitely worth me getting him to follow you when you went to see Rio. Rio is definitely a fool who would never be able to defeat you; your power is way too strong. However,' he grined evilly as he slowly walked towards her whilst forming a giant energy ball, 'you're not stronger than me,' he said as he threw a ball towards Siara. She tried to gather as much of her strength as possible and was able to avoid most of the damage. Her left arm was not able to move in time and got singed with some of her skin burning off a little.

'Argh!' Siara screamed in agony from the hit as she was flung across the room again. Drakol noticed there was white smoke coming out from her injury as it was healing.

'So you have dragon's blood in you, to heal yourself. Too bad it won't help you with this!' He said while charging at her with a fist covered in blue light. Siara knew she was not able to escape this attack. She knew that she was not going to make it. She couldn't believe that she wasn't able to find out about her mother. Where she was, what happened to her. Did she survive or was she actually dead? If she was, she wanted to go and visit her a least once before she died herself. Tears brewed in her eyes as she couldn't take it anymore.

'Where is my mother?!' She screamed in frustration.

'What?' Drakol froze, his whole body was left in shock. His mind was whirling, his blue fisted hand disappeared and instead the scar on his forehead started to hurt. 'Ahh!! What is this? What's going on? Sillia…I loved you…so much…daughter…you never told me…' He started to mumble in pain. Siara, shocked by what she just heard, used this opportunity to gather her energy and hit him with a blue light emitting from her hand. Just as she did, she ran out of the room.

On the balcony of the stairs, Siara stood there gazing at the bottom where the hall was filled with many dracs lying on the floor. Her friends all looked exhausted and hurt as well. She wanted to help them so she tried to find the strength from inside her, ignoring the pain from her left arm. She gestured with her hands for the dracs to rise to the top, slowly each and every one of them were floating in the air. She swayed her hand in the direction of the wall smashing each and every one of them into it, injuring them enough to ensure that they were unable to move. Using this chance, Siara and the rest escaped from Krark Palace and left Drakland.

Many weeks passed as Siara and the others spent their time at an inn in Fogvalor. Ming was able to get hold of more Cogolish plant after going back to the High Wilds. Siara was able to heal most of their wounds but not completely, as she wanted to. Her own wounds have not fully healed.

'I'm not going to give up on him,' Miole said as he sat on the window seat resting while the others were sitting around and talking. Everyone fell quiet.

'Who is he?' Siara asked feeling sympathy for him. She wanted to help save him too.

'He's my childhood friend, we've been together for so long. But then one day, Drakol decided to invade Waque to capture elves and turn them into dracs to make an army. I couldn't believe my eyes as I saw my best friend being snatched away from me by Drakol. He completely destroyed everything. I was barely able to escape with my life, abandoning my friend. I can't believe I didn't save him. I vowed to myself that I would save him and bring him back with me to Waque.

I just froze when I saw him. I left my friend back then and I abandoned him again now,' Miole said feeling despair and hate for himself.

'You couldn't help it, then or now.' Siara tried to console him, 'you risked your life for him and had you stayed there you would have died.'

'That's no excuse!' He yelled, cruelly punishing himself.

'Of course it is!' Everyone said. Miole looked up at the determined gazes on him.

'If you didn't escape now or then, you would not have a chance of saving your friend. Instead, you would have died and he would not be saved,' Siara said. Miole looked at her, realising that what she was saying made a lot of sense. He would never be able to save him if he died, he wasn't abandoning his friend, he was trying to get him back and had not stopped trying.

'Thank you,' he smiled at her as she nodded.

'I want to save him too!' Elpin said jumping up and down.

'Me too,' Elpina said. Ming looked at Miole with a stern look that indicated he would help him too.

'See? We all want to help you. I, for one, will definitely help you, after all the things you've done for me.' Siara said grateful to her companions.

Siara told them what she found out about her mother.

That Drakol was indeed her father and her mother was killed by him. Even though she doesn't believe it, she felt that she needed to talk to Delgar about this and decided to go back to Lastra.

'I think me and Elpin will stay in Fogvalor. We want to explore and experience new things here some more,' Elpina said.

'I'm going to stay here too. I want to be able to find out what's going on with Tolga and find any information on how to save him,' Miole said feeling determined.

'I'll help you,' Ming said, he then turned to Siara. 'I want to apologise to you. I thought you were like those dracs but you're nothing like them. If you need anything let me know, I'll always be here for you.' Siara felt overwhelmingly awed by how much Ming cared and respected her.

'Thank you,' she said getting teary, 'I feel happy hearing that.'

'Of course we want to help you too!' Elpin said feeling a little jealous of Ming.

'Me too!' Elpina said.

'You know I will too,' Miole said feeling the jealous too, 'let me know what you need when you get back.'

'Thank you Miole,' Siara said. Miole smirked at the others for being able to get her attention the most and the others glared at him. Siara laughed at their behaviour as she said, 'I'm going to be needing all of your help.' Which made them all feel needed and happy.

Siara and the others arrived in the forest near Fogvalor where Delgar had dropped Siara. She touched the pink necklace and thought of Delgar and Lastra. Just then, in the sky, a beautiful bright floating land appeared. Miole and the rest were in awe, shocked at the beautiful view and place which was said to not exist. At her friends expression, Siara smiled. 'I'll bring you all to visit next time.' They all smiled at her. Elpin started jumping up and down, excited by this. Delgar then appeared stretching out an arm and Siara crawled onto his palm. As he grabbed her, she waved at her friends who were, like Torchi, terrified of the dragon. Her friends waved back stiffly as Delgar and Lastra flew out of their vision.

'Do you think Siara will be okay with that beast?' Elpin asked.

'I hope so,' Elpina said.

'You should be careful with how you address that dragon, it could come down and eat you.' Miole teased.

'Ah! I don't want that! Save me Ming!' Elpin panicked as he grabbed Ming's arm pulling at it, hoping that Ming would hold him.

'I would have eaten you if you had called me that,'

Ming teased and Elpin screamed. Both Elpina and Miole laughed.

'You must have had quite the adventure,' Delgar asked looking at Siara who looked like she was happy to be back at Lastra.

'So many things happened,' she smiled, 'I don't know where to begin.' Siara told Delgar everything up to the point of finding out that Drakol was her father and that she believes that her mother is still alive. 'Drakol seemed confused about me though, like he didn't know that I existed.' Delgar felt a pang in his heart. He wanted to tell her the truth but wasn't able to because of his loyalty to Sillia.

'Siara…' Siara heard someone say, it was like an echo of some sort.

'Who is that?'

'Who is what?' Delgar asked curiously.

'Someone is calling me,' she said.

'Siara…'

'There it is again, who is it?' she asked the voice.

'It's me…Siara it's your mother. I need to speak with you.' Siara's heart started beating really fast. She didn't know what to do. At that moment Delgar heard the echo.

'Delgar, it's time you tell her the truth.' Delgar was surprised to hear this voice after so many years.

'Sillia…' he voiced as Siara stared at him intently. Her face was confused and her heart was still beating fast.

'What?' Siara asked shocked.

Delgar looked at her and then closed his eyes. 'There's something I need to tell you Siara,' he voiced again.

'What?' She asked, her heart leaping.

'Your mother is alive. She actually lives in Ceat,' he said. Siara fell speechless as her mouth dropped open in shock. There was a mixture of emotions that went through her, anger, confusion, joy.

'What?' She managed to whisper. 'But…how? Why didn't you tell me?' She asked him as her anger started building up.

'I couldn't! Your mother told me not to. You know dragons, we have loyalty and can't break it. I'm sorry Siara, I would have told you if I could but I couldn't.' Siara fell quiet, her mind was spinning.

'I need to be alone.' She said feeling the rage building again. She left Delgar and went outside to think about what had just happened.

The next day, she approached Delgar feeling refreshed. 'I haven't completely comprehended everything but all I know now is that I need to speak with her.' Siara said rather than greeting Delgar the way she usually does.

'I know, since it is an urgent moment.' He pointed at the pink necklace, that Siara was wearing, the crystal shone a bright pink. 'Siara,' came a soft sounding voice that vibrated Siara's body.

'Mother,' she managed to voice as her heart was pounding hard. She was feeling overwhelmed and was on the brink of tears but she managed to hold it together.

'Siara, I missed you,' her mother said. Siara couldn't respond as her heart was in her throat. 'There's so much I want to say to you but I can't do that right now.'

'I understand,' Siara managed to say, 'what is it that you wanted to talk to me about?'

'It's about your father Drakol,' Siara's heart leapt again.

'So he really is my father?' She said feeling shock and fear running right through her heart.

'Your father was never like this. He was in fact a gentle man, kind and loving. He only became like this because of this brother Daigol.'

'Daigol?' Siara asked.

'Yes. He is an evil man who hates his brother and wants nothing more than to destroy him.' Siara felt another pain in her heart; Drakol's brother wants to destroy him? 'I was able to escape because of Delgar. I was about to die and Delgar saved me by covering my scent so both Daigol and Drakol would not know that

I was still alive. When Delgar left Ceat, I told him that he needs to look after you Siara and to not let Drakol find out about you because it will put you in danger.' Siara felt a little light.

'So you didn't abandon me?' She asked relieved.

'I would never do that sweetie, you're my daughter,' Sillia said. Siara started to cry. 'I wanted to hold you so many times but I just couldn't and it was eating away at me because I knew you would be in danger if I was around you.'

'I'm so happy to hear you say that.' Siara smiled at the crystal as she was looking at her mother right now.

'I'm sorry for putting you through all this. I didn't want anything to happen to you. Delgar let you go because there was nothing he could say to hold you in Lastra unless he told you the truth, so don't be mad at him.' Siara nodded gazing up at the Elder dragon.

'So what I don't understand is how did Drakol become like that?' She asked.

'I found out while living here that Drakol is actually under a spell that makes him do evil deeds. Not only that, it was Daigol who got a witch to cast this spell on him.'

'How do you break the spell?' Siara asked eager to know.

'There is a mark on his forehead. If you make a cut on that, then you will be able to break the spell. I need you to do this Siara. I won't be able to help because he will kill me.'

'Don't worry! I'll definitely make sure to save him!' Siara said feeling excited and re-energised.

'I can't talk any longer or else it will be tracked. I'm so proud of you my darling daughter and I love you!'

'I love you too mother!' Siara said and with that, her connection with her mother was cut off.

'Are you ok?' Delgar asked feeling concerned about how she's handling everything.

'I'm fine. I'm just overjoyed at the thought of knowing that my mother is still alive,' Siara grinned.

'Well, I know you won't listen to me telling you to rest up so I guess you should just go and prepare for your new adventure.' Delgar said and Siara excitedly ran off to prepare.

Siara finally arrived in Fogvalor after feeling the nostalgia of first arriving here, she felt more acquainted with the place. She first wanted to go and visit Elpin and Elpina as she missed their cheery and carefree aura that they had. As she was walking, she sensed someone following her. Cautious of the movement, Siara went down a pathway that had no one around and stood still. 'Alright, I know you've been following me. Come out already whoever you are.' She voiced sternly as she looked around her. Siara turned around and slowly the person stepped forward. After looking at the person, she felt a little relieved, 'Tolga…' she said much softer this time, 'what are you doing here?' Tolga stepped forward, coming closer to Siara. Cautiously, Siara stood still whilst Tolga just stared at her. Emotionless and confused, it made Siara so curious that she couldn't help but ask, 'what's the matter?'

Still emotionless, Tolga didn't answer her but instead said, 'I don't know why but I seem to not want to hurt you in any way even though I've been given orders by my leader. It's strange but I feel like I don't want to listen to him anymore,' Tolga walked off. Siara blinked hard not understanding exactly what just happened, she instead continued on looking for her friends.

After searching for only a little longer, she heard a beautiful singing voice coming from the direction of crowds ahead. She knew this voice very well. It was such a calming and melodic voice, there was never a need for musical instruments. It was as though the voice resonated its own musical instruments without a need for music in the first place. The singer was very talented. She followed the beautiful melody towards the crowd and found herself watching Elpina singing while Elpin was dancing. Once their performance was over and the crowd dispersed, Siara approached them.

'Now that's something I've missed,' she said. Both

Elpina and Elpin looked at her with a huge smile.

'Siara!' They both said smiling and hugged her.

'Hey you two, I've missed you,' she said hugging them both.

'I can't believe it's been one week. It feels much longer.' Elpina said.

'I agree!' Elpin said still hugging Siara. Elpina felt annoyed at seeing how he was hogging all of Siara's attention.

'Get off her already, I've been waiting to see her for a while now too you know,' she said trying to push Elpin out of the way. Siara laughed at them. She missed them dearly, even if it was only for a week.

After they settled, Siara explained to them about what she had found out and about her mother as well.

'I'm so glad that your mother is alive!' Elpina said teary eyed.

'Me too,' Siara said feeling extremely happy. 'Not only that, I now know who my father is too! I can't believe what he's been through; he must be in so much pain.'

'No wonder he causes so much destruction, being under a spell really is scary,' Elpin said feeling saddened.

'Don't worry Siara, we'll definitely help you!' Elpina said excitedly.

'What?' Siara asked feeling surprised, 'I didn't want you to help, I just wanted to see how you all are doing.'

'We promised that we will so let's get going!' Elpin said also excited and they both dragged Siara outside to head out to their next adventure.

'Thank you, you two!' Siara said as she started walking with them. 'So where are Miole and Ming?'

'Oh they should be in Waque gathering information. That's what they last told us,' Elpina said. They headed to Waque in search for both Miole and Ming.

At the border of Waque, they saw Miole and Ming looking concerned while talking to border guards.

'What's the matter?' Both Miole and Ming turned to see Siara and grin at seeing her.

'It's been a while,' Miole said smiling at her after missing her for a week.

'You still look the same,' Ming said, even though he missed her as well.

'It's only been a week.' Siara smirked, 'I hope I am the same,' Ming smiled for a brief moment and then composed himself.

'What happened here?' Elpin asked concerned.

'Ming and I just gathered some information about Drakol. He has gone completely mad, he's lost his mind since the encounter with you. He's been going on a killing spree for a week, killing anyone that comes near him. No one can stop him. He doesn't even talk, he just growls at everyone before finishing them off.' Siara's heart leapt at the thought of her father killing. She couldn't believe he was in such a state. She needed to help him even more now. She then explained to Miole and Ming about what she found out about Drakol and Sillia.

'Wow. I can't believe that he is actually under a spell,' Miole said. 'it makes it harder for me to hate him.' Siara felt a pang of hurt in her heart at those words. It was her father who destroyed Waque and even took Miole's best friend away from him.

'That reminds me,' Siara said trying to change the subject, 'I actually bumped into Tolga when coming here.' Miole stared at her eagerly concerned.

'What? Did he harm you in any way? Are you ok? What did he want?' He started to panic.

'Don't worry, calm down,' Siara said, 'he was actually very calm, he didn't attack me. Apparently he was ordered to capture me but disobeyed his leader.'

'That's very strange,' Miole said, 'elves who are turned into dracs, cannot disobey the commands given by the person who transformed them in the first place.'

'I think that's what he was saying as well. He was very confused, it seemed like he didn't want to harm me in any way and wanted to disobey Drakol as well.' Siara said recalling back.

'What happened afterwards?' Miole asked.

'Well I was so surprised by what he said that I couldn't even help him. He just walked away from me,' Siara said. Miole looked sad at hearing this because he was not able to encounter Tolga once.

'I'm going to help you save your father Siara and save my friend,' Miole said. He thought that if he stayed with Siara, Tolga would definitely appear.

'Thank you Miole. I'm really glad that you would help,' Siara smiled.

'I feel like if I leave you alone, you're going to get into more trouble so I have no choice but to tag along,' Ming said looking away from them.

'Thanks Ming,' Siara laughed knowing full well that he would have come either way and actually cared for her.

'We might as well rest for the night in Waque and journey on tomorrow.' Elpina said as everyone agreed.

Once they entered Waque, the red fog was even deeper.

'Where is this coming from?' Siara asked as it was barely visible.

'It's Drakol's doing,' Miole said, 'he's been killing and dumping everyone in the lake in Drakland. The water is usually a dark blue but because of all the bodies, it has turned the water red from their blood. That place used to puff out white smoke that never even used to reach Waque but because of this tragedy, it has turned red. I hear it's even darker in Drakland.' Siara just couldn't believe it. The smell was disgusting and it looked horrendous. It was not like how it was when she first came here.

'My, my, my,' came a familiar voice from ahead of them, Siara and the others couldn't recognise who it was, 'what do we have here?' came the voice again. At hearing this they realised who it was.

'Rio.' Ming growled.

'You were turned into a drac too?' Miole asked

'Oh no, I wasn't turned into one,' Rio sneered, 'I became one of my own accord, which is why His Majesty has no idea that I'm here. He has no control over me. I am my own king, although I do respect His Majesty, he just isn't himself anymore these days.' Rio sighed in disappointment. 'I mean I'm all for killing but of course if I could gain something in return that would be even better. However,' he sneered at Siara, 'I do make exceptions.'

Rio approached her with a lot of speed. He aimed his fist, towards Siara but hit the ground instead. It crumbled below them. Siara was able to dodge it but the others were not fast enough. Rio smirked thinking that her speed was no match for him.

'I don't want to harm you Rio,' Siara said calmly but

sternly. Rio laughed hysterically.

'But I want you to. Come at me with your full power,' he said feeling his drac blood boiling.

'I'm not going to hurt you,' Siara said firmly.

'Hmm,' Rio smirked, 'maybe you need some motivation,' he said and grabbed Elpina by the throat. Elpina, who struggled to breathe, tried to take Rio's hand away from her throat but was unable to reach.

'Elpina!' Siara yelled, panic in her voice.

'If you don't come at me, I'll kill her and the rest of them one by one,' Rio said pointing at the others who were unable to move. Siara's blood started to boil and her eyes turned red, 'yes, that's it!' Rio said excitedly. He tossed Elpina over to the others, she was coughing and struggling to move.

Siara made scratches all over Rio with just a flick of her fingers. They were unavoidable, some of the flick turned scratches to cuts. Rio also managed to cut her but just barely. Each cut made Siara's blood boil, to the point that she was losing her senses. She smiled at the joy of harming someone. Rio felt shocked, how is she able to have this much power? He thought to himself. She was enjoying this. It reminded Rio of when he first encountered Drakol with overwhelming power. This was beyond that power. He knew he wasn't going to make it, all he could do was escape but there was no exit. He was completely trapped in her power. It was so overwhelming that the ground started to break, he was hurt without even realising it. Siara smirked evilly and grabbed his left arm breaking it; Rio screamed in pain. She had caused so much damage to him that he could feel his life slipping away. She didn't want to stop so she grabbed his leg.

'No, no, no, no! Please stop!' Rio begged for his life. Just as Siara was about to snap his leg Ming and Miole jumped onto her.

'Siara, calm down!' Miole panicked, 'You're going to kill him. Look at him, he's not moving anymore.'

'Just stop!' Ming yelled, 'we're all fine now so stop!' At hearing those words, Siara's powers simmered and she slowly calmed herself. Her eyes turned back to yellow. When she was fully calm, Ming and Miole both let her go. She looked at Rio who was unconscious on the floor, her eyes widened and she felt fearful of how she almost killed him.

'Let's take him to the hospital and get him some medical attention,' Elpin said quietly. Siara clutched her head in her hands feeling shocked about what she had done.

'It's okay Siara,' Elpina said hoarsely. Siara looked at Elpina and broke down crying while she hugged her.

The next day, Siara checked up on Rio to make sure

he was getting medical attention and was in a stable condition. Once she saw that everything was fine, she set out with the rest to Drakland. They were all really quiet and Siara knew exactly why.

'My drac's blood is strong when it does something bad, like harming someone,' Siara said calmly. She tried to break the ice with them again, 'the more I do something evil, the stronger it gets.'

'You'll learn to control it,' Miole said confidently as the rest of them nodded, 'as an elfrac, your power is very strong.'

'Well according to Delgar, elfrac's may actually be the strongest species there is. It may not be true because it's so rare. It's almost non-existent,' Siara said sadly.

Once they finally entered Krark Palace, a very heavy whiff of blood reached their noses. In front of them laid countless of lifeless bodies with their blood spewing across the hall. They could hear the growl in the middle where they could see Drakol killing someone else with a smile on his face. A shiver of fear overcame Siara as she stood unable to move.

'I was expecting you,' he growled at her, 'I have no idea what you are or who you think you are claiming to be my daughter when that's impossible but this time I will kill you for underestimating me.' Siara was not able to move as her whole body felt like it was chained to the ground by his gaze.

Just at that moment, Siara, Ming and the others ran towards Drakol trying to attack him. Miole pulled out his sword and was about to land on Drakol when another sword clanged against his, it was Tolga's. The pressure from blocking the attack tossed the rest of them away from coming near Drakol.

'What are you doing Tolga?' Miole asked, 'I thought we were friends again, why are you defending him?'

'I have no idea who you are but I will remove anyone who harms Lord Drakol,' Tolga said monotonously.

'Tolga, take these pests away from me. Just leave Siara here.' Tolga hesitated at the thought of leaving Siara behind but before he could make a move, Miole started to attack him with his sword. Tolga attacked back and pushed Miole away, taking control of the fight and moving him further away from the area until they were not visible anymore. Just as the others tried to protect Siara, they were surrounded by elves and dracs who started to attack them, only to be also forced away from Drakol and Siara.

Siara snapped out of her fear and noticed that her friends were being taken away. She tried to run after them when Drakol appeared in front of her like the speed of light.

'What are you looking at?' he said as he smacked her across the face, sending her flying across the room. Siara noticed that Drakol's hit was indeed very powerful and realised that he was too far gone and now ready to kill her.

'Drakol, do you even realise what you have done to this place?' She asked trying to distract him from trying to kill her, 'you've polluted here and Waque with a red fog because of the deaths that you caused.' Drakol did not respond. Instead he approached Siara, ready to kill her. She noticed the markings on his forehead and instantly launched herself at him ready to make the cut but instead she got his left arm.

After hurting each other for a long while, both were severely injured. Siara was on the ground unable to move, almost falling unconscious, whilst Drakol dragged his bloodied body towards her ready to kill her. Flashes of memories of her friends came into her mind and then her mother. She thought to herself that she must really be dying if she was thinking of them at this time. The thought of not being able to protect them scared her to the point that her drac's blood awakened. Slowly, her wounds started to heal and she appeared, in a blink of an eye, right in front of him. With her red eyes staring down at him, she grabbed his face with her hands and smashed it into the ground. Drakol was unable to move, Siara was able to control her blood by trying not to kill him. Instead, she made a cut on the scar, waiting for her father to be broken from the spell. Instead, Drakol's bloodthirsty eyes were still there and he was just about to attack her when he saw a large cloud of purple smoke forming behind Siara.

'Are we having a family reunion?' Came another deep voice, Siara turned around to see another drac with Sillia in his hand.

'Sillia…' Drakol had a softer voice. Siara looked back at him and noticed the spell had broken. 'I remember now,' he said gently.

MANY YEARS AGO:

'Sillia, I'm going to leave now,' Drakol said dreading this very much.

'Oh leaving already?' She asked, saddened that she would not get to see her husband for a few weeks. 'I wish I could go with you but I don't think it's safe out there.'

'I really wish you could come with me but you're right. It's not going to be a party, it's going to be a battle, after all it is Daigol.' Sillia fell quiet.

'Yeah, I just can't believe what he's doing. Killing

and torturing people for what purpose?' She voiced, feeling hurt and pained by what Daigol was doing.

'Don't worry; this is why I'm going to see him. I'll be back soon.' Drakol reassured his wife, as he gave her a final passionate embrace and left.

It had been nearly a year and Draken did not return which made Sillia worried. She wanted to go to him wandering what was keeping him but after just two months since Drakol left, Sillia was not able to go because she was expecting and didn't want to put the baby in any harm. Instead she waited for after when she had her baby to bring Drakol home and then tell him the good news.

'Delgar please take Siara and look after her it's not safe for her here in Waque. Once things are settled with Drakol and Daigol, we can bring her back here. Please keep her safe in Lastra.' Sillia said as she struggled to hand over her child to the Elder Dragon. 'Don't worry, I'm going to bring him back so I can tell him the news. Don't say anything to Drakol about the baby, I want to tell him myself.'

Sillia rested. After a few weeks, she felt well enough to move around. She finally went to Drakland where she found Daigol and Drakol in Krark Palace. Drakol saw Sillia.

'Drakol!' Sillia said feeling relieved and happy to see him. She went running to him, to hug him, when Drakol slashed her across her body. From the shock of being attacked by her beloved, she was unable to say a word. She was confused and had no idea what was going on. Why was Drakol attacking her? She was unable to move as her body and heart felt broken. Daigol, seeing the damage caused by his brother, wanted things to go no further.

'That's enough Drakol,' He said and Drakol stopped moving. Daigol was just about to grab her when Delgar came crashing into the palace.

Delgar's flared nostrils was an indication that he was about to blow. He grabbed Daigol by the throat who struggled and groaned. As he was just about to kill him, he heard a frightened voice.

'Sillia!' Drakol's voice screamed as he saw his dead wife lying there. Before either of them could do anything, Delgar took Sillia away and escaped. Daigol, at this moment took the chance to convince his brother that he killed his own wife.

'I killed her... I killed... I killed her...' Drakol repeated endlessly and each time he did, he lost a piece of his heart feeling that he was unable to go on. He screamed out in pain and lost control. He attacked his brother who then fell unconscious. Drakol's cold heart was frozen as he tossed his brother aside and ran out of the palace screaming from the pain.

Daigol managed to wake up and use the last bit of strength he had left to control a dragon. He commanded the dragon to take him to Ceat and help him recover with the use of dragon's blood.

Delgar took Sillia to Lastra where she slowly regained consciousness and started to heal a little from the dragon's blood.

'I can't stay here Delgar, my daughter won't be safe. Drakol will attack again I need to go into hiding.'

'It was not Daigol who attacked you?' Delgar asked, surprised.

'No, it was Drakol,' Sillia said with her heart breaking at every word. 'I need to stay away from him for now; I don't think he's safe. I need to find out what is wrong with him. Please send me to Ceat in hiding.' Delgar obeyed.

'I will always believe in you and listen to anything you say because you are the one that saved my kind from those dracs and let us live in Lastra. Do not worry about Siara, she will be safe with me and I will treat her like she is my own.'

Once she arrived in Ceat, she was given a pink crystal

necklace by Delgar as a form of communication. However, after doing so for a while, Sillia realised that she needed to cut all ties with Delgar and Siara as it would put her life in danger.

'I'm giving this crystal back to you. Please make sure you give it to Siara, she will need it. There will be a time when she will want to know about us, her parents and at that time you won't be able to say anything but keep her safe with this necklace.'

PRESENT DAY:

'But how did you find out?' Siara asked.

'You see, when your dear mother had her friend use a spell to communicate with you, I made friends with a few witches who were able to intercept that link and I found out that my dearest Sillia was with me in Ceat. Isn't that just fate or what?' Daigol responded with laughter. 'Now, I'm going to kill any link that connects my beloved Sillia to anyone else. That includes you two.' Drakol was just about to move when Daigol used Sillia's body as a shield, 'uh, uh no sudden movements or I'll kill her. You don't understand how much I loved her. In my black heart, she managed to make the mark of a white light inside. But she chose you,' he said with disgust, 'so I thought that if my beloved Sillia is stained by you then she has been tainted forever. If she won't love me, then what's the point of her living and me torturing myself seeing her with someone else? If she won't love me then I won't let her love anyone.'

'It doesn't work like that Daigol,' Drakol said sternly, his evil demeanour completely disappeared.

'Shut up! I don't want to hear what you think or want! I want what I want and if I cannot get that then there is no point in its existence.'

In the meantime, Siara's eyes went the deepest of red, her blood was boiling, awakening her drac's blood. Her gaze was on her mother who was unconscious and not moving. Her body moved instinctively and in a blink of an eye she was behind Daigol as she landed her fist on his face, sending him flying across the room. Daigol shocked by the speed and strength, released Sillia's hand as he went flying.

'Sillia!' Drakol yelled and grabbed her hand after snapping out of the shock of seeing the speed and power that Siara showed.

Siara, not thinking anymore, dashed across the room, not letting Daigol recover for a moment and landed another hit, sending him flying across the other side of the room. Daigol attacked her with red liquid coming out of his hand. Siara managed to dodge it and it landed on the ground causing it to melt. He flicked his finger a few times, causing Siara's skin to cut and burn.

They continued to attack each other for a while, both having been thrown across the room smashing and crashing.

'I must say you are definitely the most powerful creature I have ever faced,' Daigol said huffing and puffing. Siara landed one heavy fist on Daigol's stomach which caused him to spit blood as his body crashed to the ground smashing it completely. Siara finally reached her limit and fell unconscious.

Sillia was able to regain consciousness and noticed that Drakol is back to his normal self. She then noticed Siara on the other side of the room lying unconscious.

'Siara!' Sillia yelled in panic, both Drakol and Sillia ran to their daughter. Drakol looked at Siara and said,

'Don't worry she'll be fine, I think most of the damage is from her overexertion. She just needs to rest for a while.' Sillia felt relieved from hearing this. Daigol coughed out blood and both Sillia and Drakol realised that he was still alive. They were both about to attack him when they realised that he was unable to move and bleeding out. Sillia walked over to him. Seeing him like this caused pain in her heart. She knelt down and placed his head on her lap. Daigol was barely able to open his eyes, he felt the gentleness of his light.

'Why couldn't you love me?' He cried quietly.

'I do love you but you didn't want that kind of love,' she told him softly as her tears dropped on his face.

'The love that I wanted from you was never returned. I never received that love so I was unable to find someone else.' Daigol said.

'The way you love me, you would have found someone that loved you like that and even more. They would be there for you because you know now what love is and would have been able to return it. You always wanted to be loved by someone, it wasn't just by me but your family too. You just never saw it because you were blinded by the love you had for me.' Daigol realised now that all he ever wanted was to be loved but he was so scared of not being loved that he blinded himself with the love he had for Sillia. All he ever wanted to hear were those three beautiful, magical words, 'I have a request,' he said.

'Please tell me that you love me,' Sillia quietly cried.

'I love you,' she and Daigol smiled as he took his last breath. Sillia cried and hugged him tightly. Drakol was also crying for the loss of his brother and how he couldn't save him.

After burying Daigol in Drakland, months go by as everyone starts to move on. Siara is in Waque with her friends as she is recovering still, very slowly.

'Oh apples, I want some!' Siara said excitedly as she sees a bowl of sliced apples being brought over by Miole. 'Gimme!' she smiles stretching out her hands.

'Aren't you energetic today?' Miole said, 'maybe we shouldn't give her the apples, the sugar might get her extremely hyper. What do you think Tolga?'

'Hmm...I think you're right Miole,' Tolga said grinning.

'You guys are teasing me again!' Siara pouted as they both laughed. Elpin and Elpina rushed in at that moment.

'Siara!' They both greeted.

'We have another song for you!' Elpina said.

'I have some new dance skills too,' Elpin said, as everyone laughed. 'I learnt it from Ming!'

'Ming?' Miole questioned as they all stared at Ming trying to imagine him dancing. Ming started blushing as he glared at Elpin.

'Elpin! Stop messing around! I never taught you anything like that!' Elpin laughed.

'I wonder how you look dancing,' Siara said. Everyone fell quiet picturing the very masculine and stern Ming dancing wildly like Elpin. They all burst into laughter.

'What are you all thinking about?' Ming growled as everyone continued to laugh.

'I'm glad that I was able to remember again,' Tolga

said smiling, 'I'm happy that I remembered my friend because I was able to break that link with Drakol and be myself again, even if I may not look like myself.'

'Me too,' Miole said, 'bringing up our childhood really was the trigger to breaking your controlled state.'

'I'm glad too,' Siara smiled at Tolga who blushed, 'I made a new friend that I felt like I've known for many years.'

'How are your parents?' Elpina asked Siara.

'They are doing well. They actually visited me a few days ago. But they are busy with the red fog issue as they are trying to resolve it. I don't want them to overwork themselves by visiting me so I told them not to worry. They told me that they aren't that busy because dad gets Rio to do most of the work. If he does then he gets paid. If he tries to harm someone, or becomes greedy, his gold is taken away by Drakol and distributed to the poor.' Everyone laughs at the unfortunate situation that Rio is in because of his mischievous manner.

Siara then remembered a promise that she made to her friends and holds onto the crystal in her hand.

'Yes Siara?' Delgar's voice echoed.

'Is it possible for me to bring my friends over to visit Lastra?' She asked him.

'Of course,' Delgar said happily as he appears with

Lastra.

'As promised everyone, I'd like you to come to my home and meet my family.'

'Oh no, the beast!' Elpin said, feeling scared.

'I'm going to tell the Elder Dragon you said that,' Miole said sneakily and ran towards Lastra while being chased by Elpin. Everyone laughed.

Once Delgar brought them to Lastra, Torchi came flying past and tumbled into Siara.

'Siara! You came back! I missed you so much!' He hugged her tightly.

'Hey, hey, hey, who is this hugging Siara?' Ming said feeling protective of her. Torchi looked up to see five heads glaring at him from behind Siara.

'Ahh!' He screamed, 'Siara, who are these scary looking people?' Torchi said hugging her tightly again.

'Who are you calling scary?' Miole said feeling offended. Siara just laughed at everyone's reactions.

'Torchi don't worry. These scary looking people are actually my friends and they came to Lastra for a new adventure.' Siara said smiling. She felt overwhelmingly happy about her new life and her future that is filled with another adventure.

The Ballad of the Price Family

by Kevin Peake

2ND OF SPRING

When one is passing through Tuskbane, a necessary stop is that of the Artisanal district Auris. Complete a short journey along the side of the stream running through the middle of the area and you'll come across the small tavern hidden among the wooden forges and workshops. Often maligned for claiming beer to be their craft, yet always brimming with energy and excitement from travellers and locals alike; if you are so lucky to be there on the right evening, at the right time, you may just hear a small menagerie of lepus break out into this song as they clink their glasses in inebriated glee:

The Ballad of the Price Family by Kevin Peake

The city we live in is a right ol' mess
The farmers are leaders, the artists penniless
The council is full of bumpkin delight
They daren't show their face 'cause they're scared of a fight
Crus to the north our food do they grow,
Year-long production through drought sleet or snow,
But what do they buy to impress all their wives?
A necklace from her lover the jeweller Ash Price,

Ash Price is a legendary figure in the lepus town. He was the first to discover the gold in the stream through the middle of town and the first to engineer the technology to make the resplendent jewellery loved by the elite of the town. He was also a notorious womaniser, that song is not nearly as exaggerated as it at first may seem. The original Ash is long gone and I am all that is left of his legacy besides the business. I am Ash Price the third, current owner of Price's Jewels. My father was just as popular as my grandfather. In fact, there's a second verse to the song that I can hear being sung right now through my window.

Cormeum to the south they make all the rules,
What we eat, what we drink and even our tools!
But they won't destroy us as long as he's there,
The legendary Price, the jeweller's own heir

I haven't seen him in years. He left this life behind as soon as I could tend a forge on my own. He went off to the south with their weak watered stream and weaker political banter. The company of loose redtails was too much for him to resist, at least my grandfather had taste in the women he chased. My father sits on the council, who meet in the district of Cormeum. You have to be specially invited to get through their gates. Even the stream is blocked off. They mustn't get much more than a trickle through the barricades.

4ᵀᴴ OF SPRING

Days already appear to be getting longer, I'm ecstatic. Though I do have to pan earlier to avoid the ever eager alchemists and their immoral practices of taking whole sections of the stream floor just to get more gold. They kill everything in the river and the corpses get caught in the lining of our stream rotting, making our district a more and more disgusting place every day. I hate alchemists.

6ᵀᴴ OF SPRING

I am ever so grateful for the small book bound for me so that I am able to carry it in my pocket. If this had not been the case, my historical accounts would be lost. I had risen earlier than normal and taken my normal route to my preferred panning spot. There I panned for hours with no relent. Those blasted alchemists were nowhere to be seen and I quite enjoyed my day, returning home with more than my usual haul. That was when I saw why the alchemists hadn't bothered me; the entire district was waist high in water. How could this happen? We had drainage specifically for the stream. This should have been impossible. I made the short journey to the Crus district to find the short-eared fool of a farmer who was evidently the cause of our dilemma; perhaps a catchment had simply had a trough dug by a simple farmhand. What I discovered was an expanse of dry fields, we had endured droughts but nothing on this scale. Our lush green and amber crops had, in the course of the single day, turned black as soot and now crumbled to dust, from the lightest touch. The alchemists are to blame, surely. I will have their blood and gold for every piece that has floated away. For every hour it takes to light my furnace once more, for every page of every book grandfather and I treasured. There will be blood.

7ᵀᴴ OF SPRING

A night full of searching proved to be fruitless, no

alchemists to be found, no justice wrought upon them. A disgusting result, they surely are hiding behind the gates of Cormeum. I will find a way inside if it kills me but for now, to the tavern; I need a drink, no planning for me today.

8ᵀᴴ OF SPRING

A curious thing happened last night. I entered the tavern to find it dry, completely untouched by the devastation felt by the rest of us. I hesitantly investigated only to find no possible reason for this to be the case. The water was blocked from most homes and businesses by now but the insides are all utterly devastated. Grandfather's library, where I spent my youth, was waterlogged and collapsing in on itself. Great sections of the town were simply swept away if they weren't heavy enough and yet the tavern remains as if the water did not come near it. Were they prepared ahead of time? How? I must test something immediately.

8ᵀᴴ OF SPRING CONT.

Just as I thought, alchemist oil was rubbed into the wood to protect against patrons and their errant fluids. It can't possibly be this powerful though. I'm not the only one to come to this conclusion. The protection efforts are being hampered by so many people attempting to purchase the alchemists' oil, even now when they've all disappeared. They ransack laboratories to find them picked clean, as if they vanished into the night. All that's left are the buildings they once inhabited with their abhorrent practices.

9ᵀᴴ OF SPRING

I have discovered a new issue with the flooding of our district. There is no movement in the stream and I cannot pan any longer with the stagnant stream providing me with no gold. I must head south at once, there is nothing more to keep me here any longer.

10ᵀᴴ OF SPRING

I cannot stand the sight of the oppressive gates. The controlling air about them makes me sick and knowing the redtails are behind them when our own citizens aren't disgusts me.

'I can get you in there.' Came a voice from over my shoulder. It sounded seedy like I was about to pay far more than I should for what they were to do for me.

'How?' I asked him, 'The gates only open for the prostitutes and ministers.'

I turned to face him and saw that he was a shorter lepus. Bookish, longer ears and rounded spectacles adorned his narrow face; he had a quickness about him as if he'd been cooped up with too many chemicals. He was an alchemist. Here, at last was the target of my hatred and yet I was filled with a strange pity. Truly, I am not my father. His blood would be spilling into the streets before he'd finished a sentence if I were.

'Exactly,' he said, 'if we dress you as a redtail, the gates would swing wide open for you.' I was hesitant but as he explained the logistics, I came around to the notion. I dressed in a shawl, hood and long coat to give the illusion of looser hips; my tail was stained red with berry juice to indicate my presence as a prostitute, a sticky but overall temporary effect. The gates swung wide and enveloped me in their aura as I stepped through. I entered into the world of my father and I could not look back for fear of upsetting the wrong person. I simply had to hope I would not be immediately removed once the gates closed once more. I must make haste with my writings, there is much work to do.

17ᵀᴴ OF SPRING

Much has happened since I last wrote. I finally have an evening to myself. The drunkard I am supposed to service, has passed out from the latest tankard of beer from our tavern. I have learnt much. For instance, the tavern supplies its government contract via a cart on rails under the streams and when the good beer comes through, it's quite easy to read the documents kept by my clients. I have uncovered a letter from my father to the non-farmer members of the council plotting a coup! He writes about choking their stream to force their hand and remove them from the council. This isn't enough, he can claim forgery. I must get more evidence.

18ᵗʰ OF SPRING

My own father has gone even further than I would ever think. It's as if he knows about the letter I've found, he even appears proud that he's staging a coup. I cannot stay here, the fighting is only just beginning. I have learned all I can for now. I will escape via the railroad underneath the city. I hope I am not found.

19ᵗʰ OF SPRING

I cannot believe my luck, another night more or less to myself. This is becoming uncanny, perhaps I have an ally in the tavern. Nevertheless, I was able to escape handily but when I cried to the usual crowd, I was drained out in their song. I shall have to be smarter if I want to expose this conspiracy. I still need to fire up my furnace as well, I've barely touched my workshop since the flood.

20ᵀᴴ OF SPRING

I cannot believe the nerve of lepus in this town. I open my locked workshop door only to find not only my furnace extinguished as I had expected but my new necklaces, my gemstones and my tools had all been taken. Good thing I always have spares in my home but now I have to order new ones from Ceat and hold these ones close.

21ˢᵀ OF SPRING

Our fields, stricken as they are, are still producing food thankfully but one has to pay through the nose for anything to eat. I feel my bones beginning to pinch as I move about, my ears are wilted. As long as our district is flooded no travellers will come to buy jewellery. Surely I can find something at the separation point but that is a long journey and I am weakening by the day.

22ᴿᴰ OF SPRING

I packed up what food I could find and afford into my

coat and travelled out to the split in the stream. Only to find what used to be a heavily guarded outpost abandoned and flooded inside. I have sought refuge in a guard tower that is mostly unaffected by the water level. I'll have to explore underwater tomorrow when it's light. I don't like being here, it's unnerving.

24ᵀᴴ OF SPRING

An odd aspect of being so isolated is your mind seems to detoxify. I feel a heightened sense of clarity in my thinking. I, for one, have found the knowledge from hundreds of books far more informing than the pieces in my grandfather's library. I feel bursting with energy. It must have come from the orb.

While I was swimming around in the veritable lake created by the flooding, I happened to come across a glowing orb. I couldn't get close enough to touch it but despite giving off more light than a fire, I felt no change in temperature. There was nothing else but the orb which was giving me so much light. I could see even the deeper parts of the area, all the way up to the source, running deep into mount Ozor. The flooding seems quite odd, I could've sworn the area did not bottom out like it now does but what do I know, I'm just a jeweller. I haven't seen this area since my grandfather brought me here, ranting and raving about the dragons that hollowed out the mountain. He went mad during his final few years, going on about how he was going to find the frost dragon that lived high up on Ozor and made the water we use for everything. That its scales were golden and its blood ran strong. A drop could grow a mighty oak. He even claimed to hear it roar from time to time. It's a shame to see the once great minds of the elderly go to waste.

25TH OF SPRING

I was followed here. I found a pack cast aside near the tower full of salted meats and breads. No mercenaries eat this well unless they killed a merchant on their way here. I'm not complaining about getting some proper nourishment, rather than the dwindling meagre supplies that I brought with me.

I have an idea to retrieve the orb. Theoretically, if I use the pack and weigh it down using some rocks nearby, I can use it to drag the orb to shallower water. I just need to be careful of the mercenary following me is all. From now on, I'll sleep with one of the many daggers strewn about the tower.

27TH OF SPRING

It fell right in front of me. The unmistakable arm of one

of my kin but where did it come from? Surely whoever was hired to follow me has not resorted to siege warfare tactics. After all, I am in an unlocked tower for the majority of the day. It's very strange. Nonetheless, I appear to have enough rocks to weigh down the pack sufficiently. I shall make an attempt tomorrow.

28TH OF SPRING

I have it! I am actually holding the sacred glowing orb in my lap as I write this entry. Its beauty far surpasses anything I have yet seen of this world, not even grandfather's finest work compares to its beauty. I feel a strong urge around it, to crack it open, to pierce its perfect exterior and drink the knowledge that emanates from its inside. It feels a waste to pervert such beauty but I must know what is inside.

45TH OF SPRING

I do not know what happened at the source. I do not know what happened to the 'orb' of which my daughter speaks. I do not know what happened to my daughter but whatever she did returned the stream flows to normal. Our family jeweller's is no longer waterlogged and I have returned to the business of making the finest jewellery available. It feels fitting to add my experiences to this collection since I know better than anyone what happened in Cormeum. I had to leave her, if I didn't have my say for the Artisan district, the farmers would have had their way with us all and ruined my heritage and legacy. I wrote that letter to rally the last of the artisans on our council to say no. I did what I had to in order to keep my daughter safe and instead she pens such vile things about me and scatters the pages in the wind. Had I not collected them who knows who else would have? It's been 2 years since her passing and I miss her every day. I am grateful, however, to be reminded of her every time the locals finish their favourite song.

> *A fiery woman did ever I see,*
> *Had time for naught but her jewellery,*
> *When the flooding began did she sit there and cry?*
> *Course not! Ash Price fixed all that were awry!*

\- Collected with love by Ash Price II. Former councilman of Tuskbane.

Telling the Future
by Alexandra Ispas

The gates of stone towered high above their heads. With eyes of wonder, the young elven witch admired the old castle-like building before her. She found it hard to believe she was actually facing Ceat, the great city meant for witches. She suddenly forgot how she even got there. That was not important anyway. All she could think about was how amazing that place was. Then, her tutor suddenly ruined it for her by saying:

'This is as far as I can go. Non-witches are not allowed inside.'

'You can't be serious. Are you really letting me go alone Traffo?' The disappointment could be heard in the young elf's voice.

'I came with you all the way here but I can do no more than that. I am confident you'll find the rest of the way on your own. You're an independent, beautiful, young witch, Dretha. You just don't realise it yet.'

The witch didn't know what to say. She was both sad this was her parting moment with Traffo, her old and wise tutor but also flattered by his compliment. She simply remained silent and continued to admire the stone walls and wooden gate that blocked the view of the inside of the magical city. She stared so hard that one might think she was trying open the gates with her eyes only but part of her didn't want them to move at all. She wanted time to freeze so she wouldn't have to part with Traffo. While she was not paying attention, he patted her auburn hair which always upset her but this time she almost ignored it. The whole point was to get a reaction from her but she seemed impassible, enveloped by awe and left staring, forgetting all that surrounded her.

'We can go back if you want...' suggested the old elven tutor.

'No!' she snapped, suddenly returning to reality. 'I want to be here.' She now looked toward her tutor with wide eyes of promise and continued on a sweeter tone. 'After I finish my studies in magic, I'll come back to find you.' Traffo laughed shortly with his rough voice, making his wrinkles more obvious than they normally were. His reaction left her confused but she said nothing in reply. He only pushed her closer to the gates.

With uncertain moves, she took a step forward and

then another until she could lay her hand on the little door carved in the large gate. She shakily turned the knob and opened the door. Immediately she turned around, hoping she would now be prepared to tell Traffo good-bye. But he had already vanished. She knew that he always had his secrets but the way he had suddenly disappeared left her dumbfounded, unable to understand how he could have done that... or why. Dretha felt deeply disappointed, lowering the corners of her rose lips in sadness.

Slow and uncertain, she made the step that would decide her future. Dretha was now within the borders of Ceat but her mind was elsewhere while she closed the wooden gate behind her. Deep in thought, she was soon disturbed by a foreign voice.

'Hey! You're a newbie, right?' shouted a voice from behind her. Dretha turned around in a startle. She started walking slowly towards the voice she had heard, unsure who had spoken. It sounded like it came from a young girl such as herself but she saw nobody around. 'What, don't you see me? Gosh, you need a lot of training!' spoke the voice again in an excessively playful tone.

'Who are you?' questioned Dretha as she turned round and round in confusion, not sure what was happening. She couldn't even admire the beautiful stone city because of her desperation to find the one addressing her. 'Why can't I see you?'

'Because of magic, that's why. I'm right here,' the stranger said and Dretha felt a touch on her shoulder from behind. She jumped in surprise, turning around quickly. Without a second thought, she sent a wave of flames before her. Both of them were equally shocked by the happenings but the stranger witch was the one harmed. She was now in sight, on the ground, licking her burnt hand. She seemed to be an elf too and even of similar age but with wider eyes and golden hair. Dretha didn't feel sorry for the burn she caused but apologised out of mere politeness.

'I didn't mean to do that, I'm sorry,' she spoke in a soft voice as she helped the other girl on to her feet. 'Don't scare me like that next time.'

'Ouch. And there I thought you weren't a witch. Your fire is strong, what else do you know? Wait, come with me to the healing house and tell me on the way.'

'Um, alright.' Dretha had nothing better to do, so she accompanied the strange witch to the healing house, somewhere within Ceat. She tried to remember the way but it all seemed so complicated at first. The other girl told her at some point that all new witch apprentices started with a tour of the city. On the way they spoke, Dretha finally answering the other girl's question. 'I'm good with elemental spells mostly. I used to make use of them around the cottage where I lived with my tutor.

When the weather was too warm, I would make wind and when it was too cold I would start a fire.'

'I guess you like fire since you use it with so much ease.'

'Well, I don't know. It's unpredictable.'

'Like you?'

'I suppose...' Dretha hesitated, unsure what to make of the other girl's response but she continued as if nothing had disturbed her. 'Anyway, what spells do you normally use?'

'That's a hard question... my favourite is by far invisibility but I usually cast spells of levitation. Do you want to fly?'

'What? No!'

'Haha, I was just kidding. What's your name?'

'Dretha.'

'My name's Menigel.'

'When did you first come to Ceat? You seem very familiar with everything.'

'I am because I came about a year ago. I came a while after my older sister got here. She once sneaked out of here just to tell me how amazing this place was. I didn't know anything about magic then but I'm a quick learner so I decided to come visit. It turned out I never left.'

'Your sister?'

'Graniel. She's quite famous here. You'll like her. I

think she'll be your guide tomorrow actually.'

'How can you be so sure?'

'Because I want you to meet her.'

'That doesn't answer...'

'Come, the healing house is right around the corner! My hand still hurts...' spoke Menigel and then whispered to herself: 'I need to learn some healing.'

Dretha was left following in silence. She found it hard to say too much around Menigel who was so hyper and always had something to say. In spite of the pain Drethel's burst of flames had caused her, she was still full of joy and that almost scared the inexperienced witch. Still, she was quite glad to have found someone to talk to. It was probably as good a start as any. Upon arriving at the healing house, she was kindly greeted by the healing witches who told her to drop by at any point if the need arises. One of them happened to be Graniel. She was a tall elven witch with golden hair just like Menigel's, except for the darker hue. All in all, Graniel was a more mature version of her younger sister, regarding both appearance and mentality.

Menigel was quick to find her place in her older sister's arms and seemed to have forgotten all about Drethel for the time being.

'Sister! You have time to heal me, right? Can you teach me your magic too?'

'Easy, easy, Menigel. Don't be so rash about things.

You need to calm down before you can learn any healing. What happened to your hand anyway?' Graniel looked concerned when her eyebrows met in a frown but Menigel was not disturbed by her sister's reaction.

'Oh, it's just a little burn. It's no biggie. Accidental fire. Hey, can you be a guide for my friend here? She's new. Her name is... uh...'

'Drethel. I'm Drethel.'

'It's nice to meet you Drethel. Did you just arrive?' kindly asked Graniel.

'I found her at the gates!' immediately spoke Menigel, not even leaving the new witch any time to respond.

'What were you doing there? You know you're not allowed so close to the exits!'

'Nobody saw me, I promise!'

'You used invisibility again, didn't you?' There was disappointment in the healer witch's tone.

Menigel suddenly stopped talking and looked down. Her older sister seemed indeed upset as she mended the girl's wounds. Using the opportunity, Drethel spoke:

'I just arrived a bit earlier. I'm a bit overwhelmed by this place and I don't know the surroundings, where to go and what to do.'

'Don't worry,' spoke Graniel with a sweet and caring voice. 'You can stay over at our place tonight and tomorrow I'll show you around and help you figure everything out. You will get a strict schedule which you must follow and you will have to learn all the rules. Always be careful not to break them.' After the brief explanation, Graniel turned to her wounded sister. 'There you go, Menigel. Be nice and take your friend to our home. It's getting late and small girls like you ought to be sleeping at this time of the day.'

'But it's not even late!'

'Menigel...'

'Okay, okay, we're going, we're going.'

After huffing and puffing on the way out, Menigel started leading Drethel towards her and Graniel's home. It turned out to be a stone house, no larger than the cottage Drethel had lived in with Traffo. She almost felt at home there.

'Normally new witches who don't know anyone yet or who are of the same family will stay in the same house, two by two. Tonight is an exception because you arrived too late to see the Head Mistress so you can stay here. Ohh, I'm so excited, we can have a party tonight, just the two of us... Graniel won't mind, I'm sure. We will dance and we will laugh...'

'Menigel, Menigel...'

'What?'

'I think I should rest tonight.'

'Oh...' All cheer from the playful witch vanished in a moment.

'It's already dark. Just tell me where I can sleep.' Exhaustion made Drethel feel overly serious, something that wasn't in her nature at all but in comparison to her new friend, she seemed much more mature anyway. Especially now.

'Follow me,' responded Menigel in a low voice. She seemed sad but there was nothing that could be done about it. Drethel felt no guilt.

As soon as she could, the tired newbie laid in her temporary bed and closed her eyes, falling asleep on the spot. Overnight she saw troubling things. Things she had been seeing for the past few days but as scary as they were at first, they now seemed quite normal, almost pleasant. Not once were they identical but there was always one element to unite them: fire. Everywhere she looked there had to be at least ashes, a spark or a flame and whenever she looked at her hands they were on fire.

Tonight she dreamed that she was watching a field from above. She watched from a castle probably but she couldn't be sure. She must have been on the rooftop but not allowing herself to look toward the building. All she knew was that it was immense and that surrounding it was a barren field with occasional stone buildings in ruin. All vegetation having turned to ashes and no living being daring to wander around willingly. Only two or three creatures could be seen mourning. Their faces were marked by the hot weather, ready to pass away themselves because of asphyxiation. Their tears had run dry but their sobbing went on until they were left with one last breath of the intoxicating air. Further away on the horizon, she caught merely a glimpse of dark orange liquid but that was when the dream faded away.

Drethel woke up in a gasp, this time sweating. It was still dark outside but she decided to get up and wander around. She needed to take a breather and calm down. She wasn't disturbed by the sights in her dreams but rather by the fact that she felt pride in watching the dead scenery. Something was wrong with her lately. She refused to think about it during the day and made sure nobody would find out. If she was good at something, that was causing accidental fires and hiding things. The thought worried her.

As she sneaked out in the chilly air, she made sure she didn't wake up the other two witches in the house. The sun was about to rise, so she wasn't all alone but none of the other witches minded her. She noticed how there was nobody guarding the roads, like she remembered seeing in her hometown during her early childhood years. But that was so long ago. Seeing no security, she expected Ceat to be a place where all witches felt at home and that thought, at least, encouraged her.

Telling the Future by Alexandra Ispas

The streets were sometimes narrow and until the sun rose higher up on the sky, above the towering stone walls surrounding the city, she remained in almost complete darkness. Sometimes, however, she arrived on the main streets which were wider and more circulated. They were also lit up better. Most buildings in the area were identical, one-story stone houses placed seemingly at random. There were, however, taller and more elegant buildings like the healing house but also tailors and other shops selling food and potions. These buildings grew in numbers as they neared the castle right in the middle of the stone city. That was apparently where everyone was going, so Drethel decided to go there too, ignoring the fact that Menigel and Graniel were probably searching for her worriedly.

Only upon entering along with everyone else did she speak, in theory to herself but someone had answered her whispered thoughts.

'Where to now?'

'You should probably go see the Head Mistress.' Drethel turned to see a female maikong in robes of vibrant colours. She seemed calm, almost smiling but serious by nature. Seeing the young girl's confusion, she went on: 'I'm Mrs. Flareth, the elemental spells teacher. You're not one of my students, so I assume you're new.'

'Yes,' was all the girl could muster to speak. She was stunned to see, for the first time in her life, a maikong female and even more, one dressed in witches robes. It was quite a beautiful sight. Drethel tried not to stare. As she followed the teacher around the foreign corridors with towering ceilings, beautifully carved stone pillars and colourful tapestries, Drethel kept thinking about the elemental spells teacher who she stumbled upon. She seemed to move smoothly like the course of a calm river, yet sure like stone. She was silent like the wind and active like a flame. The young girl felt like she was already starting to like that teacher and not only because she taught the use of elemental spells.

'Did you come here alone?'

'No,' responded the girl, finally awakening from her daydreaming. 'I came with my tutor but he's an elven alchemist so he couldn't join me inside.'

'I see. Did you arrive overnight?'

'I got here yesterday afternoon.'

'Oh! Where did you rest then?'

'A girl my age found me... her name is Menigel. I stayed at her place last night.'

'Menigel? Graniel's sister?' Drethel nodded. 'She's quite the figure, at least during my class. Always full of energy and ready to make a joke. She's so young and innocent I can't blame her but it's a pity she won't pay attention most of the times. You need to be patient with her if you want to get even a conversation going.'

'I noticed. She's quite talkative and full of energy.'

'You seem her opposite.'

'I'm not actually... well, not entirely. I'm just shy at first. And a bit overwhelmed by this place and all the new things and people I meet.'

'I'd give it time if I were you. Just go with the flow and everything will seem natural before you know it. We're all a family here, so don't worry about mistakes. Everyone is here to learn, just like you. Here we are! The Head Mistress's office. Let's go in.'

And in they went. Of course, the teacher did the talking, presenting the new witch whose name she didn't even know. 'Drethel. I'm Drethel,' said the young elven witch as she stared the Head Mistress in the eye. She was an elven witch as well, just like most witches around there, including Menigel and Graniel. Her robes were even more spectacular than the maikong teacher's ones, with delicate golden lining, or so it seemed and she wore a pointy hat that brought a shadow on her serious face. It made her hair look black but Drethel wasn't sure if it was just the shadow playing tricks or not.

Upon leaving the office, Drethel had been given a schedule she was to inspect later. For the time being, the maikong teacher explained what came next for the day. First of all, the newbie witch would have to wait for an advanced apprentice to guide her around. The first day, she was told, she wouldn't have to go to classes but the activities would sum up to something even more exhausting. Together they were to go visit the tailor and get some robes similar to those the other apprentices were wearing. Only afterwards was she to be presented Ceat and all its wonders, buildings and gardens alike. It turned out that at some point, only if she was considered mature enough and felt like she had too much time, she could get a job in one of the buildings around Ceat. Just like Graniel who was working every evening at the healing house because she was best in healing. Thankfully, it was indeed Graniel who guided the girl around. This was a fact which made her feel much more comfortable, knowing already that she was a warm person who she had already met. She had to admit that complete strangers frightened her at first.

The day passed quite quickly since she was continuously kept busy. Drethel felt almost drained of energy but had just enough of it left to walk towards her new house where she met the witch she would be staying with. To her surprise, she was a drac, quite older than herself but cheerful to see a new face. Drethel didn't exactly feel scared after Graniel's departure, leaving the newbie and the drac witch called Ash-kay all alone. Although that was now Drethel's house too she still felt for a while that the drac witch was the proud owner and that she was intruding her space. Maybe it was the greyish skin or the somber look on the drac's face that gave Drethel that feeling but whatever it was, she tried to avoid letting her hesitant feelings show.

After a short while of awkward small talk, Ash-kay showed the young girl to her bed and she quickly fell asleep but not before making sure the other witch living there had left the room and closed the door. If it would open, she would wake up. The first night was tense and the dreams were quite alike as well:

Drethel saw herself again somewhere high, or thought those were her eyes watching anyway. This time, she dreamt of falling, something which was new. For minutes she fell, until she reached a busy marketplace. Everything was made of stone. Deep within, she knew why there was stone and nothing else but the clear explanation was still foreign to her. The doors, the windows, the vegetation, it had all burnt so long ago. Only the stone walls remained. The people didn't seem bothered. They didn't mind her falling either which was annoying. They were walking right into her as if she wasn't even there, causing her to fall to the ground because of the impact. When they were about to step on her, that was the moment her fury showed up. In all directions, there were blazed ribbons of flames, setting everyone on fire. For a moment they seemed unaffected and as Drethel stood up, she thought they really couldn't see or feel her but it wasn't the case.

They stared for a moment as if they were dead people remembering they were actually still alive. Then when they realised their clothes were on fire, they started running chaotically, bumping into each other and spreading the dancing flames. It felt strange how there was no sound, only dynamic images running through the girl's dreaming mind.

The door opened all of a sudden and Drethel woke up in a startle, unsure if it was the dream or the door that woke her up. Ash-kay was staring at her in curiosity from the hallway, not daring to come in. Drethel stood up and stared back, not sure what was really going on. She had no idea that some witches had the power to share others' dreams. Still, that remained a secret because of the lie the drac witch spoke.

'You shouted. I thought something happened. I guess you had a nightmare.'

'Sorry,' replied Drethel without showing any sort of emotion. She was still recovering from the dream. 'I didn't mean to scare you. I didn't have a nightmare. Sometimes I just talk in my sleep,' she lied, quite sure it wasn't true but unable to prove it either. Maybe she did talk in her sleep sometimes, just that Traffo had never told her.

Ash-kay nodded and left, closing the door slowly and with shaky movements that luckily Drethel didn't notice. Never before had the drac witch allowed someone with such dreams to sleep in her house before. She knew that Drethel was special somehow but she needed to study her dreams more before she would understand how exactly. Soon, surely, Drethel's dreams would reveal a possible future, provided all pieces of the puzzle were laid on the board correctly. So far, the future was quite frightening but the drac witch found it rather exciting. She liked the young newbie. Her dreams at least.

'Maybe I've found my partner after all,' Ash-kay whispered to herself before going back to sleep. Her thoughts were on the future. A future where she was in power with Drethel as her right hand.

Two witches, an elf and a drac, ruling together. If not for Drethel's disturbing dreams, Ash-kay would have imagined the picture herself but the young witches' dreams were probably more accurate anyway.

Ash-kay was patient. She knew she had years to wait but she had a burning feeling within her that the right moment would arise. 'Wait and the time will come,' she told herself every night starting with the one when Drethel made her appearance.

Song of the Redwoods

by Tomas Marcantonio

The woods look smaller than they used to, Ara thinks to herself. It used to seem as though the great redwoods swallowed up the whole sky, their loaded branches conspiring with the wind to create a whirling ceiling of emerald green. Before she left, the High Wilds was the whole world. Now it is just a garden tucked away in the universe's back pocket.

The smells, at least, are the same. The smoky scent of the red bark, the wet perfume of the moss, the bitter mesh of the ferns that blanket the forest floor. The cold clear roar of the river swirls in the mint breeze; she can taste every bend, the swelling rhythm of the current, the flinty descent of the gravel that swims along the riverbed towards the heart of the forest. These were the smells of her childhood; the smells of a past life, all rushing back now like a collision of crystal shards piecing themselves together inside her chest.

Dusk and the light is fading. The tree huts will light up soon, green balls like firefly tails awakening through the dark, glowing along the rope bridges that string the redwoods together in a living, breathing network of moss-drenched peace. The lighting of the lamps was always Ara's favourite time, when her mother used to come back from her adventures in the wilds, bow slung over her shoulder and the river's icy glare still reflected in her eyes. But that was a long time ago.

Now Ara picks her way through the green web of the forest floor, every fibre of it reacting to her slow advance. The ferns tremble as her fox tail brushes their leaves, as though they can sense her new magic. She steps carefully over the violet and crimson fungi and listens to the scratching of the redwood beetles that scuttle to and fro up the bases of the trunks. Her steps are light, almost silent; now she is as much a part of the forest as the trees themselves. Her fur of burnt almond could have been woven from the threads of the hanging vines; her ears, short and sharp, are browned, furry leaves that shiver with the early evening breeze. The honeyed fire of her eyes pierces through the twilight like a knife through wet earth. She is home.

High above, the singing has started. Ara hears the baritone harmonies of the greying maikong males, their slow choruses heavy in the canopy. Their voices vibrate through the boles of the trees, the beat of Barrow's great drum drawing them on. Ara will be greeted like a hero, the long years of training and solitude finally complete. She is no longer the distant youth who skipped through the forests alone, re-enacting the great hunts. Now she is truly a courier of magic, the pride of the High Wilds, one of their own.

She comes to the base of the redwood which she knows better than all the rest. There's something about the scent of its bark; a thousand memories stir as she lays a paw on its trunk. Looking up, she sees movement high above. The lamps are being lit. Her mother will be there, waiting for her with those sharp, feline eyes that have greyed with age like the fur on her neck. Ara begins the slow climb up the ladder that she watched her father build when she was just a cub, still on all fours.

Every step is slow, measured. She feels the forest breeze on her tail, senses her father's musk on every sanded rung. The singing grows. Ara can even recognise some of the voices: her uncle Roan, his aged and throaty bass; her young cousin Bell's sweet, untrained soprano. Barrow's great drum echoes through the gathering night like the forest's own heartbeat.

She has longed for this. She remembers the moonlit nights in her high tower in Ceat. The great castle did not just house magic; it breathed it through the very stone of its walls. It was alive, its marble floors glistening with possibility, the long halls and winding stairwells and hidden passages singing with whispers and lullabies from another world. For the other girls hoping to be trained in the art of magic, the castle was home. For Ara, it could never be.

She yearned for the long woods of her childhood, the green-leaved sky, the river that pulsed with fierce silver life. Every night at the window of her tower, she looked out upon the rampaging ice-turquoise waters that circled Ceat, imprisoning her and she thought of home.

Now here she is, ascending towards the understory of her childhood. And it is only now she knows she will not stay. She realises now, with her paws on her father's ladder, that The High Wilds cannot be lost. Her father is gone, along with the best of the maikong warriors. The numbers in the trees are dwindling and the voices that chorus in the canopy have either sung too many songs or too few. The maikong don't need another girl to walk the rope bridges selling spells while the trees grow old and their bark falls away like autumn leaves; they need a leader, someone young and able to fight for their cause.

Ara sees the glowing eyes above her now. The river-shell trumpets are being blown; the homecoming call.

Her journey will start soon, Ara is sure. But first there is this night of emerald lights and the maikong choir that whistles through the trees and the wet eyes of her mother and a celebration.

∗∗∗

Night holds the High Wilds in its palm, engulfs it. Dancing has swept through the trees; the frolicking of the cubs, the sombre waltzes of the last ancient families. Barrow's drum pulses through the blue night, his great arms as steady as the mountains that lie beyond the woods. He nods at Ara as she passes him, retreating from the crowds.

She picks her way through the great swathes of maikong who have come to celebrate for her. Each one bows as she steps past them on the wooden bridges; the older maikong put their paws to her neck and declare how proud they are of her. She thanks them all, not knowing what to say or how to behave.

Ara only stops when she is alone, standing in the nest of The Umber, one of the oldest communal trees. She absorbs the room, her eyes drawn to the moss-kissed chairs. There are pictures on the walls of the great maikong of the past. She breathes in and closes her eyes; the scent of her uncle Roan's leafy tobacco fills her nostrils, the spiced aroma of aged oak. She remembers sitting in one corner when she was a cub, watching her father, uncle and the maikong leaders smoking with their legs up on the log tables, laughing their deep laughs. Back then, she thought nothing could ever touch them.

'They're asking for you.'

Ara turns to see her mother standing at the entrance to the hollow. She's aged only a little in Ara's absence; her grey furs are still outnumbered by brilliant reds. She stands upright, a shawl draped over one shoulder where her bow used to be. Her eyes are still sharp, still knowing.

'This was father's favourite chair,' Ara says, one paw perched on its back. 'Somehow I always expect to see him here. A roll of leaves in his hand and smoke passing across his face.'

Her mother smiles. 'Shall I tell them you'll be along later?'

Ara shakes her head and takes a last look around. 'Let's get it done.'

Her mother stops her as she moves to step outside. 'You learnt more than just magic in Ceat,' she says, scanning her daughter's face. 'I know that look; tell me.'

Ara observes the piercing glare in her mother's eyes. She had hoped to leave it all unsaid, at least for a while.

'The councils are gathering at Fogvalor,' Ara says. She doesn't need to say anymore; her mother knows what it means. Elves from the mountain refuge of Waque and the long-eared lepus from Tuskbane, the river city, moving together at last. Beyond them all are the Slay Waterways, the home of hot stone and the red flame.

'We can't be left behind to watch our forests burn,' Ara says.

A cloud seems to pass across her mother's face. The lights in her eyes diminish.

'Tomorrow,' she says simply. A smile appears at the corners of her mouth but it's forced; it's the same smile she used to give Ara when she used to ask when her father would be returning home. 'We'll talk about it tomorrow.'

In silence, they walk back to the commotion in the central web, arm in arm. Bell comes skipping around them as they make their way into the circle at the centre, where Roan steps forward out of the crowd. He's supported by a gnarled blackthorn walking stick but he still has strength in his back, his chest still barrel-strong like it used to be before the warriors marched away that night the fighting began.

'A song,' he says to the crowd, 'from our Ara.'

He bows, puts his hand behind Ara's neck and touches foreheads with her. Ara steps forward, her throat dry. She tries to smile and pulls her cousin Bell into her side. Aware of hundreds of pairs of eyes on her, she begins to sing, her mezzo-soprano drifting up into the canopy.

> *Their songs are carried on the wind*
> *Heather and dogwood call*
> *Their message on your distant road*
> *Here's shelter from the squall*

Bell joins in with her soprano, Roan with his deep, earthy bass.

> *The redwoods sing above the rest*
> *However far you roam*
> *Cross mountains and the river wide*
> *The trees will bring you home*
> *Cross mountains and the river wide*
> *The trees will bring you home*

The last note lingers in the air above the crowd, the three voices joined in the night like creepers entwined around a tree. When they fade, the maikong bow their heads and put their paws to their hearts. For a moment all is quiet and then the wind responds with its own sweet tune. Ara closes her eyes and feels the cool night on her fur, hearing the rustling of the leaves. When her eyes open she's greeted with smiles; paws are placed on her shoulders. Her night is almost done but she will leave the crowd with something to remember before the music and dancing resume. Closing her eyes, she whispers under her breath, sensing the magic pulsing through her veins like the rush of a river. Raising her paws like she's summoning the wind itself, she channels the energy of the forest like sunlight through a prism.

She can't help but smile at the responses of the crowd.

'Look!' comes Bell's voice but everyone has already seen. The trees around them explode into colour: jade, cherry-rose, mulberry, poppy, honey; then marigold, cranberry, caramel and crystal. The trunks of the redwoods glow like engorged fireflies and collisions of flowers explode like fireworks towards the canopy. The maikong cubs jump up and down, trying to catch them out of the air.

Some of the adults clap and cheer; Ara's mother puts an arm around her daughter.

'That will have drained you,' she whispers into Ara's ear. 'You'd better rest for the night.'

It's true; Ara can feel the effects of the magic already. Even within the safety of the castle in Ceat, she never used her magic unless she had to. She can already feel the weakness in her arms and legs, the difficulty catching her breath. But it was worth it just to see their faces. Bell interlinks her elbow with Ara's and together they move through the crowds who were still excited, exclaiming at the new beauty of the High Wilds. Ara's homecoming is complete.

Then the scream comes. It pierces the peaceful night like a shard of glass. All maikong eyes turn to the river.

'Please, Ara, tell me this is just more of your magic,' Ara's mother says to her ear.

Ara sinks to her knees. There, beyond the river, a mountain of fire. The trees are burning, engulfed in crimson flames. A charcoal cloud of smoke mushrooms towards the canopy, growing by the second.

'They're here,' Ara says. 'It's started.'

***

Panic spreads through the understory. Children cry for their mothers, families run, hand in hand, adults call for their loved ones through the crowds. Ara turns circles, expecting someone to take charge. If only her father were here, or any of the warriors of her youth. She looks to her mother, the strongest spirit she knows; her eyes are fixed on Ara, set, believing. Ara knows her time has come.

'Take Bell,' Ara commands.

Her mother nods, pulls her daughter's forehead into her own. 'I'm proud of you,' she says.

Ara nods and watches her mother leave with Bell under her arm. Ara runs over to Barrow, his mighty body suddenly dwarfed in the crimson light; his pepper-grey face is dark with terror. She nods to him and he pounds his great drum. Silence descends upon the treetops. For the second time tonight, Ara steps forward when she would rather retreat into the shadows.

'Tonight,' she says, her voice raised. She can hear it shaking through her throat. 'Tonight the maikong don't sleep. We all knew this night would come and now it's here. We will not hide in our hollows and pray for the world to pass us by or sit dozing in our armchairs like moles blind beneath the ground. This is the night the maikong wake. The night we fight for the place we love.'

She looks over the faces in the crowd. There's fear in every pair of eyes. As she speaks, the poisonous smell of smoke grows. Fur glistens in the approaching glow of the fire. But no one is telling her to be quiet. Everyone is listening.

'The old, the weak, the young,' she says, 'retreat, as deep into the Wilds as you can. Anyone with magic, get to those fires and bring them down. Anyone who can fight, with me.' She casts her eyes over the crowd. Too many cubs, too many weathered bodies held up by walking sticks. The maikong warriors are no more.

'I'm with you,' Barrow declares, the drumsticks still in his hand.

'And I,' says an auburn-furred female, barely older than Ara.

Ara nods at them and several more step forward. There are no warriors among them, no great magic users, either but they each have a fire in their eyes.

'For the trees,' Ara says, holding a hand to her heart.

'For the trees,' the maikong chorus in reply.

'Let's go,' Ara commands.

They take off like a wind through the canopy bridges, towards the smoke, the heat and the burning bark of the redwoods. Ara feels the strength returning to her legs; she'll need every ounce of it she can muster.

'There,' says Barrow, pointing to the forest floor a hundred metres ahead. There's movement in the underbrush, flashes of silver light. 'dracs,' Barrow says.

'No,' Ara replies. 'Not dracs.'

She leads them at a run down the wooden walkway that coils around The Mother, the oldest and grandest tree in the forest. Descending, the heat of the forest floor intensifies. Ara hears Barrow's coarse breath behind her, the lighter footsteps of the younger maikong in tow. Ara stops dead at the bottom; a bow raised in the arms of a creature of white fur, an arrow nocked, ready to fly.

'You maikong have become slow,' she says.

Ara holds up a paw to keep Barrow and the others behind her.

'Put it down,' the white creature commands to someone over Ara's shoulder.

Ara turns to see one of the adolescent males behind her with his bow already raised. Ara nods at him and returns her gaze to the arrow aimed at her face. The lepus is taller than Ara by an inch, her long ears standing on end, alert. The leather cuirass over her shoulders and chest is light, washed brown. Her fur is white all over, her eyes blue like ice, cold and fierce. She keeps them fixed on Ara when she speaks, her voice low and clear like a storm.

'Would you let spiders eat out your eyes while you sleep in your trees?' she says, unblinking. Behind her the fire continues to rage. 'Where are your warriors and witches?'

Ara hesitates. 'This is us.'

The lepus casts her eyes over the ragtag group Ara has assembled. 'My comrades have chased a group of dracs back across the river but I sense there are more. What do your noses tell you?'

Ara nods. 'East,' she says.

'Yes. The rest of my party are fighting your fires; I suggest you assist them.'

With that, the lepus lowers her bow and turns, her long-legged strides disappearing into the underbrush.

'Barrow,' Ara says, watching her go. 'Take the others and get those fires under control.' She turns to face him, observing the greying rings beneath his dark eyes.

'Why are those blasted rabbits here?' he says quietly.

Ara knows the drummer's misgivings. But the days of skirmishes between the maikong and the lepus are done. The elders may not like it but now they wake to the same dangers.

'It looks like they're saving our forests,' Ara replies and she takes off after the flashes of white ahead, her head low, ferns whipping against her face as she breaks through.

***

The lepus is crouched behind a rock that's hardly big enough to conceal her body. Ara slides in next to her and places a paw on the wet stone. They're on the edge of a pond of spruce green, smelling of damp cattails and lichen and algae left to fester. The lepus doesn't flinch when Ara arrives at her side; her eyes are fixed straight ahead beyond the line of trees on the other side of the pond. Mayflies dart silently across the surface of the water.

'What is it?' Ara whispers.

'Dracs,' the lepus answers.

Ara sees them now, the shape of the dark elves. Their red eyes burn through the soft light of the forest floor, their horns like acacia thorns above their ears.

They move swiftly, lightly; not part of the forest like the maikong are, Ara thinks, watching them; more like part of the earth itself, as though they have burst through the muddy ground like dry roots coming to life.

'From the Slay Waterways,' the lepus says, 'home of the red flame. On the first night of this moon, they laid waste to the artisan district of Tuskbane. Since then, my party have been tracking them.'

Ara watches them; she counts three, low to the ground, foraging among the weeds.

'Where's your weapon?' the lepus asks.

Ara shakes her head. 'I returned this night from Ceat.'

The lepus turns to look at her for the first time. 'Then let's see how much you learned there. What's your name?'

'Ara.'

'Vyne,' the lepus says. 'Follow my lead, Ara.'

Ara watches Vyne, her long ears now tucked behind her head, twitching subtly like flames in a breeze. Her snout is short, her nostrils contracting and expanding. Her icy eyes are fixed ahead, unblinking and wide, adding years to her youthful face. 'Now,' she commands.

Vyne leaps upon the rock and extends her body in one swift movement. She unsheathes an arrow from the quiver on her back and nocks it with practised dexterity, her expression unchanged. She releases the arrow before the dracs are even aware of her presence and Ara watches it sail through the air, fast, unquivering, cutting through the darkness like a shooting star. It strikes the body of the nearest drac and the dark elf falls backwards into a bed of wildflowers. The other two scamper off in opposite directions like ants at the first drop of rain.

'With me,' Vyne commands to Ara, who feels suddenly naked without a weapon in her hands. Vyne leaps from the rock to the edge of the pond and takes off through the wood. Ara follows her at a run. The drac ahead of them is short, clattering through the scrub with a wild, bug-like gait. Vyne unsheathes a second arrow and sends it through the leaves but the drac weaves to the left as though it knew the shot was coming. It turns into a thick tangle of vines and ferns and out of sight.

'Ara,' Vyne says, looking over her shoulder.

Ara leaps up the closest tree, scrambling up the branches like she used to do as a child. She finds her feet on a branch ten feet above the ground and sees the brown scuttling movement of the drac ahead. She closes her eyes, channels the magic through her body; the wind rushes through the trees behind her like a tidal wave, flooring ferns, making whirlwinds of fallen leaves, bending the thinner branches and sending swarms of insects into the air. The wind floors everything, an unflinching surge but it passes through Ara's body as if she were not there, like a ghost revisiting her childhood home. Ara opens her eyes and the wind dies suddenly, like a bird falling dead from the sky.

'There,' she says, pointing to the spot where the drac is scrambling back to his feet. 'Twenty yards.'

Vyne is still below, already back on her feet after being taken down by the wind herself. She leaps forward, nocks another arrow and looks up to Ara. She keeps her eyes on Ara's extended paw and points her arrow in the same direction, trusting Ara's eye. She doesn't flinch or even blink as she releases the arrow, nor when it hits the leathery body of the drac, now floored once and for all.

***

'Impressive,' Vyne says, plucking her arrow from the body of the fallen drac. 'I'd heard that the castle at Ceat was no more than a relic these days. The young lepus who return from there have little to show for it apart from tales of frivolous youth.'

Ara looks into the empty eyes of the drac. 'I spent much of my time alone,' she replies.

Vyne looks back down at the creature on the floor. She places her foot on its side and rolls it over onto its front.

'We should find the other,' Ara says.

Vyne shakes her head. 'It will be halfway back to Slay by now.' She looks up to the canopy. 'The fires are diminishing for now but the dracs will return.'

Ara drops to her haunches.

'The magic weakens you,' Vyne says.

Ara nods.

'I hear it takes time,' Vyne says. 'I envy you. I tried to learn and when I was a little younger than you but I never took to it. This is all I have.'

She strokes the tip of her bow, that was now, slung over her shoulder, almost absent-mindedly.

'What can I tell my people?' Ara asks. She looks up at the Lepus, her white fur bright and sharp in the darkness, her long body lean and strong. 'We have no one to lead us.'

Vyne keeps her eyes on the canopy. 'It seems that you do,' she says and then she takes off, slowly into the trees. Ara follows. 'When the fires are put out, set up sentries at your borders. Elders will do, any who know your forests well. We move for Fogvalor when the sun rises.'

'Who?'

'My party and yours. Choose two you can trust and meet us at the mouth of your great river at dawn. The journey will be long.'

Ara looks at Vyne's face. 'I've only just returned,' she says and she feels foolish as soon as the words dissolve into the air between them.

'And next time there may be nothing here to return to,' Vyne says, returning Ara's gaze with that cold stare.

***

Dozens of trees have been lost. Ancient redwoods that stood long before the maikong ever made their homes in the western woods; giant sequoias with hollows so large that great feasts used to be held in them; camphor trees so stout and hardy they had looked to Ara as though they would stand until the end of time. The sky is still dark at dawn, the air thick with smoke, hanging like a black ceiling over the canopy of the High Wilds.

'How long will you be gone?'

Ara's mother is standing at her shoulder, watching the edges of the sky lighten. Ara shakes her head.

'I expect for some time.'

Her mother puts a paw on Ara's shoulder; their eyes meet.

'I'm sorry to leave you,' Ara says, 'so soon after returning.'

'I'll still be here when you get back.'

Ara nods and two figures emerge from the trees behind them. At the front is the young female who stood by Ara's side the night before; auburn-furred, wiry, with narrow, slanted eyes; an apprentice witch.

'Without her, we would have lost a dozen more of the old camphors,' Barrow told Ara when they returned that night after fighting the flames.

Behind her is the young male who was quick with his bow; his fur dark grey like the smoke through the canopy. They both nod at Ara, unblinking. Ready.

Vyne's party are waiting at the river. Ara looks once more to the canopy above; there's peace now in the early morning light, the hazy green mist of the awakening forest.

'You'll need to be ready the next time they come,' she says.

'We will be,' her mother replies. 'As long as we're here, not a single leaf of the High Wilds will be harmed. We'll see to that.'

She holds a paw over her heart; Roan leans on his stick by her side, Bell next to him with shining eyes. Barrow is behind them, stony-faced, sending a muster of crows into the sky with the first beat of his drum. All of them watch on as Ara and her companions make for the river. The elders blow their shell horns and the sound echoes through the understory; the rest of the maikong emerge from their hollows, standing on the rope bridges to watch the departing youths.

Ara walks out in front with her companions at

her side. Impressive. That word from Vyne still nestles somewhere within her, adding volume to her shoulders, straightening her back. The night is finished and Ara's adolescence dissipates with the rising of the sun. The day begins.

Bell begins to sing; a moment later the whole forest is in chorus.

> *The redwoods sing above the rest*
> *However far you roam*
> *Cross mountains and the river wide*
> *The trees will bring you home.*

The Lepus Saviour

by Alexandra Ispas

'Tell us another story, we want another story, Papa Lepus!' screamed the lepus younglings.

'Another story...' The old lepus spoke in a low voice, seemingly deep in thought. He had been watching the sky while having spoken.

'Something new. Tell us a new story!'

'Do you want to hear... the myth of the Island of Lastra?'

'Yes!' they all shouted in unison.

'And how the island is said to be moving at will on the Ocean of Korwa?'

'Yes!' The younglings were getting louder.

'And how it is said that every hundred years it reaches shore in search of young apprentices, like you? And how the lucky ones to find it are bestowed with remarkable gifts of magic and eternal happiness...'

'Yes! Tell us, tell us more!'

'Well, that was the story.'

'Nooo, Papa Lepus, don't be like that. Tell us more!' they pleaded but in vain.

The old storyteller from the northern part of Tuskbane started laughing in a hoarse voice as he scratched the back of his ear, an old habit of his. The younglings were gathered around him, waiting for an exciting story. They started shouting, hoping that would get them what they wanted. They kept jumping around the place, hugging each other or finding comfort in Papa Lepus' furry arms.

'Alright, alright,' finally spoke the old storyteller and suddenly there was silence. His low and calm voice was enough to make the small ones stop and listen, their big eyes wide and sparkling with curiosity as they stared up at him. 'But this is the last story, for the night has come and your mothers must be worried.'

'We promise, Papa Lepus!' they said in unison, full of excitement, knowing that their elder had saved the best story for last. Only a few moments later, after complete silence had found its place among them, when there was only the wind blowing, the river running and the crickets singing, that was when the story started. At first in a low voice and rising as the excitement grew. The lepus elder was indeed a remarkable storyteller.

'High up in the mountains, there once lived

some peculiar creatures that kept to the shadows. Down, on the fields, there lived the happy elves of Waque, dancing and singing during the day... but weeping at night, for the creature in the mountains would howl like this!' As the storyteller imitated the terrifying sound, the children gasped audibly, in fright themselves. With a voice just as scary, the story went on: 'The big and angry dragon will come to eat you!' Again, the children gasped, hugging each other. If not for the shadows made by the dancing flames of a nearby fireplace, the effect might not have been so piercing but Papa Lepus knew how to tell a good story. He used his shadow to make the dragon come to life. 'And as he howled, the dragon of the night flew above the city of the elves, watching for those foolish enough to come out at night.'

'Did uncle dragon eat the elves?' asked one of the smallest lepus children in a sweetly terrified voice as he curled up in his sibling's arms. Their ears were all flat on their faces, as if that would save them from their fright.

'Don't be silly,' spoke another. 'Everyone knows dragons don't eat elves! They eat salad and carrots.'

There was a laugh a few steps away from their small group. Another lepus was listening to the story but from a distance. As he was older than those younglings, he preferred to stay alone but listened nevertheless.

Now, however, he approached the group with small jumpy steps when Papa Lepus addressed him:

'Laluo, why don't you tell the rest of the story?' The lepus called Laluo smiled, taking a deep breath as he sat next to Papa Lepus and took the role of telling the story but before he got the chance to say anything, an eerie sound could be heard in the distance.

'Is that... horses?' asked Laluo, a little on edge. They had no horses anywhere near Tuskbane. The lepus were not ones to tame wildlife and ride other creatures to their own will. Those were dracs and that meant trouble. 'Kids, go inside!'

Sensing the older ones' discomfort, the young ones started to panic as well and that caused them not to hear what Laluo had said. They jumped in each other's arms and crossed paths as they tried to get away, causing them to fall flat on their furry back and bellies. When their parents started rushing over, the real chaos started. Now the dracs were in sight and the lepus children would only listen to their parents, who were desperately making their way to get their children, always finding time to give Papa Lepus a very upset look for keeping them on the streets so late at night.

There weren't many to leave for security before the dracs on horseback arrived. Laluo and Papa Lepus remained where they were in order to make sure everyone was safely inside but there was not enough time for that. When the ill-intended dark elves were already beside them, the children were still exposed despite the efforts of their elders. In the midst of chaos, the young ones were caught by the ears and thrown in some sacks, disappearing completely from sight. Seeing how it was night time, it was harder to figure out who was missing, who was safe and who was still in danger.

This chaos was short lasted, however, as the horses never stopped and moved quickly through the streets. The dracs riding them were getting a hold of all the lepus children they found. Other than the still-echoing sound of the horses' hooves, cries of loss filled the chilly night air. Everyone went back to their homes, knowing there was nothing to be done and silence enveloped the northern Tuskbane. The wind was howling in symphony with the water splashing from the bountiful river but the crickets stopped singing in fear themselves and that left the atmosphere dead and desolate. That is, until Laluo spoke in a low, yet hopeful voice.

'What do we do now?'

'Now? Nothing. It's too late. You should go to sleep,' answered Papa Lepus, already starting to walk toward his own home. Now that the excitement of storytelling and the cheerful response of the kids were both gone, tiredness and old age were hard to miss on his face.

Laluo was left staring in awe, not believing what he had just experienced. Never in a million years would have he ever imagined that a squad of dracs would come riding to steal their young for who knew what dark purposes. Even worse, nobody meant to do anything about it. A fire started burning within him, a fire he never knew existed. As he faced the way the impostors had come and left, he was set on doing something. He wasn't quite sure what but surely a solution would come to mind overnight. Now was the time for rest. He had a feeling he was going to need every bit of energy he could gather. And time. He didn't know how much time he could spare.

Unfortunately, there was little rest he managed to get, so before the sun rose up in the sky, he was already preparing to leave. Riding seemed to have been so convenient for the dracs that came and left like the wind. Too bad he would have to make do with his feet alone. At least he was a quick-footed lepus and that was a reassuring thought. The fields, he knew by heart and the Slay Waterways were, he knew, somewhere to the north. There were just fields until that uncomfortably burning land. At least, that was what Papa Lepus' stories would tell him about that place. No creature dared get too close. Now, he was aiming to reach its core and at this point he felt no fear.

All of these thoughts rushed through his mind like the river flow, all while he was packing up. It was sad he would be alone but all great stories started with lone wanderers seeking adventure and they ended up happily ever after. He would like that too.

Nobody had woken up by the time he was already out of Tuskbane and too far to be seen with the naked eye, as big as a lepus eye was. He decided that starting with a quick pace would prove fruitful in the long run and short rests would be accompanied with a carrot and a biscuit for dessert. Over the day, he passed by several lepus villages and sometimes overheard conversations about how their young had been stolen as well during the previous night. Who knew how many lepus children were in the hands of the dracs or why but whatever the reason was, it couldn't have been for a good cause. Some asked Laluo on what business he was stopping by at those villages but he would always come up with a vague answer, saying he was looking for a good story to tell. He was well aware that if word was spread that he was heading for the Slay Waterways, they would force him somehow to go back home. He couldn't permit such a thing, therefore he took no risk.

Only upon exiting the last lepus village the following day was he stopped by a worried lepus mother who had somehow sensed his intentions. She seemed full of energy, jumping in place and with a basket on her back that was full of enough provisions to last a week. Laluo knew she was going to be tagging along no matter what he told her, so they stuck together through the journey with little to no complaint. Her name was Lumao.

As it got darker, they were nearing their destination, until they eventually started to catch a glimpse of the Slay Waterways somewhere downhill. The city was lit up with torches at every street corner and seemed full of life even then. That made the two lepus wonder how busy it could have been during the day and they suddenly got worried. Getting there was no big deal, especially since the weather was mild during the day and slightly chilly at night but now... now what?

'Heroes in stories seemed to have it so easy,' whispered Laluo as if to himself.

'Stop living in a daydream. This is reality. We'll stand watch tonight and tomorrow during the day so we can analyse their patterns.' Lumao was set on business. If not for her plan, the children might not have stood a chance to be saved.

'At least they can't see us up here. Hey, do you see that too? Hide!'

'What?' But before Lumao had the chance to understand what it was the other was seeing, she was grabbed by one hand and forced to sprint her way until the cover of some bushes. Of course, she complained her fur would be getting all messy and that her head was spinning from the sudden rush but Laluo silenced her. That made her sigh and listen after having rolled her wide eyes.

'I heard hooves.' Hearing his words and putting the pieces together, Lumao froze in place like a statue, her hairs on edge, making her gain in volume in a very funny way. But now was not the time for jokes. 'Had we stayed there, they would have seen us. Let's follow them.' Slowly, Laluo went out of their hiding spot and in perfect silence went back to the top of the hill to get a better view.

'You're crazy,' whispered Lumao but followed him nevertheless, her ears lowered in fright.

Now they were both watching the Slay Waterways, careful not to lose track of the drac riders that had nearly seen them. Of course, their sacks were full with movement which was clearly the lepus children trying to get away. They both gasped, as if they had expected anything but that. The drac squad they had seen was entering the city which was surrounded by stone walls, protecting the wooden buildings built on stone and rock waterways. At least the second part of that place's name was applicable to reality. Even better, all water was covered with a layer of mist, hiding all that rested within it, including the ripples at the surface.

'At least we know how to get in and how to move unnoticed,' spoke Lumao confidently.

'I hope you're not talking about the waterways.'

'I am, why?'

'There are Slark swimming in the water, not to mention you're going to boil in there.'

'Your stories again...'

'This is no story.'

'Very well but what do you suggest then?'

'I think...' Laluo thought the situation over and over but came up with seemingly nothing. 'I think that entering through the waterways is a solution...'

'See?'

'I didn't finish. I meant to say that we can't move around through the water. It's the most dangerous place you can be in within this world.'

'Fair enough.' A pause followed but Lumao spoke again, this time with a tremor in her voice: 'Does it feel to you warmer than on other nights?'

'It is.'

'Can't wait to feel the heat of the day...' sarcastically spoke Lumao, making Laluo laugh slightly.

While they spoke, they kept watching which way the drac riders were going, hoping to memorize the way so that they could follow their footsteps when given the occasion. At least they seemed to be taking ways less patrolled from within the city, at least at night. They were also poorly lit up, making it hard to see clearly even with careful lepus eyes. As the two looked down to the city, they often lost sight of the dracs only to find them somewhere completely different. They were aware that they would need a lot of luck to reach their destination well and alive. Getting out was a whole other story and seemed worth thinking about only after having finished the first stage. Laluo, at least, was slowly become more fearful that he might not make it to the end well and alive, or would be caught and tortured in the process. Lumao either didn't show it or didn't feel it, because she seemed perfectly calm and glad to have even a glimpse of a plan in her head. She had hope and nothing to lose.

They ate and rested well, being woken up by the scorching sun as it rose on the sky in a seemingly sudden motion. They waited a few hours under the shade of some shrubbery until it was darker and cooler outside. Only then, after having eaten, they began sneaking their way into the Slay Waterways. They decided it would be a good idea to leave behind their provisions for when they would return with the saved lepus children. They only hoped it wouldn't take too long to get in and out but at least there was no extra weight to drag them down. Also, once they were inside, wet and complaining of the heat, they figured out how great of an advantage they had for being small. In addition, their fur was luckily quite dark in colour, so they easily blended into the shadows of the night.

Thankfully, Laluo's hearing was very acute and Lumao's sight was also well developed to seeing in the dark, so whenever a drac would be nearby, at least one of them would notice and they would hide. Being a lepus made it easy enough to sneak around as they were not only small but also silent as the night wind. Nobody noticed them for as long as they roamed around the mostly empty streets of the Slay Waterways.

The harder part was deciding what the right way to go was. Lumao had paid much more attention to the path they had inspected the previous night, yet Laluo kept contradicting her. That caused them to lose time and wander wound in circles for a while, until another squad of riding dracs passed by. They hid and watched, immediately following, only to discover they were already very close to their destination. Lumao seemed in perfect control of her emotions, although the anxiety to see her child burned in her eyes but Laluo... he was growing in tension by the minute. He knew it would only get harder until the end and that was no soothing thought. The dracs had nearly seen them and they still had no idea how to get inside the building where the hostage kids were being held.

'Hide, someone's coming out,' whispered the female lepus when she noticed the door knob moving. They immediately hid and watched. The squad of dracs that had passed them by a little earlier was now coming out, full of satisfaction and ignorant enough to leave the door slightly open. While they reached for their seemingly restless steeds, the two lepus sneaked in, hoping nothing unfortunate would await them on the other side.

The room was empty. Well, there was plenty of furniture, which would make it convenient to hide but it was free of any living soul. However, the floorboards, creaked audibly even under their light lepus paws. They froze in place when the door closed all of a sudden, making a very loud noise in comparison to the silence they had grown used to while in that city. They instantly turned their heads to see who had closed it, thinking it had been slammed from the inside. After a quick but horrible moment of tension, they realised that the door had been closed with force from the outside and they took a deep breath. They moved on.

With steps as silent as possible, they moved little by little and stopped to listen every few seconds. The room was seemingly empty and that was strange because they were surely in the right place. At first sight, the room made the whole building, as there were no stairs to a higher or lower floor. On the other hand, Laluo heard in the background some low volume weeping. It had to be the kids but where were they? In the furniture, no and yet they searched every closet, every drawer, every wooden box and chest but there was nothing of interest, except for a ring of keys hidden at the bottom of a barrel, under a badly folded cover. Lumao had figured that a cover's place wasn't in a barrel and that rose suspicion that led her to finding the keys in the first place. Upon moving the cover out of the way, she noticed the keys, lots of them. There were probably around twenty, small keys filling up the space on the key ring. They were for something, surely.

'I think they hold them in cages,' she said before showing Laluo what she had found. Almost at the same time, he spoke as well.

'They can't be at a higher floor, since there is none but I think I found a trapdoor leading to the basement.'

'That's good news!' each of them said, somehow in unison. Of course, they didn't like the idea of the children being kept in a basement, locked in cages but they were positive they had found a way to reach them. Well, almost. Now they were searching for that trapdoor and of course found it after having moved the furniture around. The gloomy room made it quite a challenge but they did it in the end.

'Mama!'

'Laluo!'

The kids immediately took notice of the two coming down into the basement and started screaming their names and making a whole lot of noise. There were many who didn't know either of the two lepus coming to find them but were just as happy to know they would be rescued. It was all that mattered and in order to make it happen truly, they even kept the silence when told to.

'Be patient, I'm getting you all out of here!' said Lumao in a low, yet excited voice, calming down the kids while she worked her way with the keys. Laluo kept them under control not to run off and silenced them, explaining how it was crucial they do not do anything foolish. They seemed quite scared behind the sudden burst of hopeful joy. Who knew what those dracs meant to do to them, or what they had been told was going to happen, in case they had been told anything in the first place. Whatever the truth, it didn't matter. They had to get out.

'How did you get in?' came a whispered question from one of the lepus kids. He didn't ask 'How did you find us?' Laluo started to answer the child's question.

'No, I mean, how did you get in here? They put someone to guard the door.' The two rescuers' fur stood on end, as they exclaimed in unison and disbelief 'what!' All kids nodded. Getting in might have been easy enough but getting out was going to be a problem.

Laluo looked around in frustration, hoping that a path in that gloomy air would show itself and save them a whole deal of trouble. Of course, it wasn't the case. He was feeling the panic from his quick and nervous heartbeat but forced himself not to let it show because of the kids around. He was the rescuer after all. They expected him to have thought everything through. He couldn't allow himself to make those kids lose what little hope they had. Whatever it took, they would get out of there safely and live their lives happily back home with an exciting story to tell. He promised to himself he would make that happen. The question was how.

'Alright, let's go,' spoke Lumao after having unlocked all the cages and freed all the younglings. 'There's a window next to the exit, we can check if the drac guarding is really there.'

'I'll go first and check,' said Laluo with a mask full of confidence. 'Wait for my signal. Until then keep quiet.' Everyone nodded as they looked at him with their large shiny eyes.

Careful not to make a sound, Laluo went up to the main floor and neared the window next to the door. At first it seemed like he were staring into emptiness because of the dark night but soon he started making out the shapes of the buildings and the road. There was no living being in sight. In order to let the others know the road was clear, he jumped just hard enough so that those underneath would hear an empty sound in the ceiling. Soon enough there was movement. As organized as those children were in a time of despair, their large number and horribly synchronized steps made it seem like chaos. At least they managed to keep the silence as much as possible. The floorboards didn't creak under their especially light steps and that was by itself more than enough.

Before opening the door, Lumao checked the window herself. Laluo figured out that she didn't trust him so much, although she had said nothing about it. Then, seeing with obvious surprise that indeed there was nobody guarding the door, she tried the knob. In vain.

'It's locked!' gasped the kids and immediately they started making a fuss about it, which was harder now to stop. Lumao still tried:

'Listen, listen! We can break the window and get out.'

'But they will hear the noise and see the damage and then they'll come after us,' spoke in a breath one of the kids.

'He's got a point,' enforced Laluo.

'What do you suggest then?' Lumao was mad at Laluo and was having a hard time hiding it.

'I think I know a way!' said one of the kids. All attention was diverted in his direction now. Immediately he explained. 'We have to go back down. I think I saw the entrance to a gnome tunnel.'

'But this makes no sense! What would a gnome tunnel be doing in a place like this? There are waterways everywhere.' Lumao then had to take a deep breath to calm down. The situation was getting out of control now. Laluo felt no better but still stayed calm.

'I say we at least go and see. Maybe we'll find our escape route.'

And so they did find it. Hidden behind all sorts of wooden objects that they had to move out of the way. Small in a corner was a tunnel waiting just for them. Lumao insisted she lead the way, so Laluo agreed to stay last and make sure everyone was safe. Until they reached the other side of the tunnel, they were all safe. Too bad the tunnel was short and they didn't get too far but at least they were outside. It was still night and best of all, there were no dracs around. It appeared they had reached a riverbank. Knowing the course of the water, Lumao knew to lead the way in the right direction, content she wouldn't get lost from that point. It seemed almost too simple.

Laluo hoped she was finding a secure path and wasn't leading them all into more danger but there was nothing he could do in this matter but hope for the best and play his role as guardian in the back. Therefore, every two seconds he would take a peek behind and check if there was anyone in sight. He couldn't rely on his ears this time because as silent as the kids might have been, their steps could still be heard if you paid a little attention. The ground was vibrating in a very soft, almost unnoticeable tremor. It was all his ears managed to focus on in such a time of crisis.

They continued for some minutes, to the point where the children thought they were lost. It was hard to keep them quiet now and even worse, they were starting to see dracs, making their every movement dangerous. Lumao was having a harder time finding a safe path and there were no other miraculous tunnels and even fewer places to hide. Laluo noticed, as he kept a permanent eye on the dracs who were coming and going out of his sight like flashes, that they were all in a rush. At that hour? It was still night time. He got worried, especially when he heard someone speak dangerously loud. It was Lumao, trying to get her message across to him who was all the way in the back.

'I found an exit!' Of course she meant a waterway that exited the city. The kids would have to get wet in order to exit that place but they all seemed fine with it.

'Run!' said Laluo, knowing that at least a drac must have heard them talking by now. They were close to the exit, so they could make a run for it. As long as they weren't followed outside the city, they would all arrive safely back home. In order to make that happen, Laluo knew he would have to remain behind. As the children and even Lumao followed his impulse to run, they didn't look back to notice him gone. They wouldn't miss him, not for now.

Laluo took a deep breath and started running but

in the opposite direction. His plan was to let the dracs think they had exited through the wrong waterway and cause them to waste time searching for the larger prey. Thankfully, his plan worked perfectly and since he was a quick lepus, the chase seemed to go on forever. Still, minutes after the exciting chase began, he was caught and the dracs figured out it was only a diversion. They knew it was too late to chase after the ones who had escaped as they were surely too far and would soon get back to safety. They had one and a big one. That made them satisfied enough for now.

Laluo was beaten until he blacked out and then thrown in one of the cages meant for the lepus children. He had no idea and dared not wonder what would happen to him but knowing that he had accomplished his goal to set free the young ones, he felt victorious.

He was now a hero and they would start telling stories about him.

Laluo was at peace.

The Journey to Ceat
by Nisha Hamilton

'Spirit! I feel like we are close!' I excitedly said, though looking at the exhausted black cat made me lose excitement. How could he be tired? The magic is coursing through this area, I feel it through me! 'Spirit!'

'Yes! Yes, I'm here. Your go-to companion... forced to be here! Travelling... you know.' The black cat groaned his words, complaining 'Not knowing when we could ever end and take a break. No... of course not.' I rolled my eyes at his response. He's so terrible at travelling; I don't know why mum made him go with me. I'm responsible! I can perform basic spells, besides I'm going to Ceat to make myself better at magic! Spirit doesn't even have magic! He can talk because of a magic spell from mum. It's like she doesn't trust me.

'I get it, you're tired. But I'm telling you, we are

close!' I answered back. 'It has to be here somewhere.'

Spirit sat down, establishing his stand on this situation. 'Here in the forest... a huge kingdom of witches resides,' Spirit groaned. 'Look, Annette, I've been there with your mother and... let me tell you... this is not the place.'

I faced the cat and sat down to mock him, 'Well you don't feel the strong magic coursing through you. You wouldn't know what I, a witch, am feeling at this very moment. What might you say about that?' I smiled, knowing he cannot argue back. I saw his eyes squint, defeat is it?

'I don't... but you don't know the personal experience I've already encountered,' Spirit argued back. His head tilted up, in the joy of his victory.

I groaned, 'Fine!' I threw myself back and landed in the grass around me. My back aches as I haven't stopped travelling for days. Having this small rest was worthwhile. 'Then how can we find it? Everyone has denied us! They declined our questions.'

Spirit walked up to me, I felt his fur brush against my clothes. I felt a pressure of two spots on my stomach, then the pressure evened itself out. I looked to see Spirit laying on me. 'Not everyone accepts witches, you know.' I set myself up, making sure he wouldn't get uncomfortable in the process. 'Your mum had to go to Ceat. It wasn't a perfect adventure for her as well.'

'What do you mean?' I asked.

Spirit hopped off, I looked up to see the sun is already setting. I haven't set up a campsite yet. 'I heard that a true witch will find it in a time of need. The rumour has been true for your mother, I doubt you would be any different.' He curled into a ball next to me. I had to sit and reflect on the idea.

Mum took this journey and tells me stories all about it, especially of how she met friends and witches just like her. She learned almost every ingredient for potions; she started creating her own spells on her journey! She never told me about the dangers on her journey, she never even told me where to start. Once she got to Ceat, she was one of the most famous witches. She knows every spell, perfected even the most complicated of potions, she created her own inscriptions in witchcraft. Why is it she won't teach me the complicated spells? She sent me with Spirit to fend for ourselves, she didn't want to help me with complicated spells. Why would I go to Ceat if I have the master of magic as my mum? Madame Medea's heir, the one and only witch descendent of Medea, forced to travel with a nagging cat and low food supplies.

I had to stop. This anger is filling me up. It surely was not supposed to be like this, it just came out as such. 'A true witch will find it in a time of need...'

Spirit's words. He meant every syllable, though he was tired. I'm getting closer, I know I am. I sparked a small fire onto some nearby twigs and covered myself with my cloak. We'll continue travelling tomorrow. I'm close to showing mum, that I can be the best witch to ever surface! A few more steps till I make it!

I rose quite early, as I always do. I shook Spirit, trying to wake him up. He, of course, didn't budge. Like a rock, he is deadly still. Could he be dead? Did I accidentally kill my mum's familiar? I took a closer look. Looking for any signs of life. I stared so closely, mortified in case I had done anything to hurt him. I inched a little closer. Spirit's chest expanded and shrunk. He was still breathing.

I exhaled my own still breath and grabbed a charred branch from the fire earlier. I turned back and threw the branch at the sleeping cat. It wasn't a big branch, though just enough to feel it. 'Wake up!' I yelled, the cat woke up on the twig's impact and ran right over to me. He looked up in fright, his face immediately turning into disgust at my sight.

'You are a cruel witch, you do realise.' His grumpy voice echoed in the forest. He trotted next to me as I bent down to pick up my brown satchel. He jumped in, as he usually does and I took out my broom. 'Your broom?'

'I've been thinking...' I bent down and carefully put my satchel over my head and shoulder. Spirit hopped out as soon as I did. 'If we want to reach our destination, we can't walk forever. Maybe we can find it quicker this way!' I happily picked up Spirit and let him climb into my bag, seeing him trying to get comfortable once again.

Spirit crouched down, 'I don't think that'll get us any closer if you don't know in the first place.' I put the broom in between my legs. 'Though, this beats walking any day.' his soft purrs vibrated my bag.

I readied myself. 'three... two...' I took in a deep breath and exhaled, 'one!' I ran forward and jumped into the air, soon flying upwards. I am still shocked that I can fly by myself. While I was home, I couldn't get off the ground unless mum had helped. I ripped through the leaves and popped out of the top of the trees. I felt the breeze fly past me. I smiled at the small achievement, I did this! I'm doing this! I'm controlling this! Though, mum had always warned that flying on a broom drains some of your magic energy. I felt the broom draining me already, though I didn't let this stop me. I'll continue flying until I can't stand the tugging feeling. I looked down at a fluffy face smiling in the wind. This feeling is incredible, I couldn't stop that feeling so quickly.

It was exhausting on the broom, though it made me realise the purpose of this journey. Ceat, the best place to train and become the greatest witch! Surely, the adventure would teach me the dangers and how to prepare myself in case of attacks. I'd be ready for anything Ceat throws at me! However, there's usually no fighting in Ceat. That journey sounds more like an archer's journey, the Elven status of archery was essential to their customs.

This journey would teach me all about my own strength and ability to adapt! The journey would show how a professional witch would react to the shortage of food and how to survive by herself. Yes! Surely, mum wanted to prepare me for the worst possibilities. Though, it's a bit strange to have me fend for myself. Especially since I don't know how to start.

The draining feeling had grown stronger in the few hours I've been flying. I looked below me to find a huge flowery meadow, filled with colours and sunlight. I lowered myself and soon reached the bottom. I opened my satchel to find Spirit sleeping, I guess it's a silent walk for me.

The silence was interrupted by a rustle behind me. I didn't see anything running when I took an aerial view. I reached for my wand, I do know a protection spell in case of emergencies. I shouldn't speculate that a noise is a threat, though I shouldn't take my chances all the time. My wand looked like a simple twig engraved with my name and some decorative swirls. I wanted to be just like my mum, so of course, my wand needed to be personalized like hers.

My wand came from my belt holster. I took a firm grip and turned around. I came face to face with a boy. He had greyish skin and pointy ears like an elf. His eyes were not like mine though. His hands gripped a wand as well, only shinier and decorated with jewels. I took another look at his face, seeing his eyes widen like mine.

'What are you doing?' I asked firmly. I felt my bag move, I must've shocked Spirit by the abrupt turn. The boy in front of me looked at my attire rather than back at my face.

'Are you a witch?' the boy asked, I squinted at his notice. How could he ask when he is being interrogated? Can't he see that my wand is pointed at him?

I gripped my wand a little stronger. 'What were you doing? Trying to kill me? Why do you have a wand?'

The boy chuckled a little, 'Hey, no need to interrogate.' He put his wand back in his holster and raised his grey hands in the air. 'I'm safe. See?' He reached for his satchel and dropped it. He did seem safe in my eyes.

I lowered my wand, showing trust as I would a

normal civilian. Though, I wouldn't have threatened a normal civilian at wand's point. I felt my bag move and become lighter. I saw Spirit hop out and stand beside me. 'I'm Annette and this is my companion, Spirit.'

'Who's he?' Spirit sat down as if he didn't want to meet him in the first place.

'I'm Damien. I've been travelling for a while, it has been too long since I've seen another face.' Damien picked up his bag and slung it around his shoulders. 'Seems you two have been travelling as well.'

I smiled at the question, 'Yes! Oh if you'd seen the gnomes and lepi that we've encountered, you'd be shocked by them. The lepi ears are so long!' I went to explain more but I felt a pressure on my boot. I looked down to see Spirit look up at me, shaking his head no. I rolled my eyes and looked up at the new partner in crime. 'There are more stories though, I'm still travelling. How about you join us?' This feeling, something took over me and I couldn't put my finger on it. I felt warm and fuzzy about this encounter, this was meant to be.

Damien's eyes widened again. 'Really?'

'No!' Spirit yelled out. Damien and I looked down at him. 'Annette, what do you think you are doing?'

'Your cat is talking.' Damien hissed under his breath. I quickly smiled in apologies and picked Spirit up. 'Is that a spell?'

I chuckled nervously. I felt a weird feeling talking to him. It must've been the overwhelming joy with trusting another person. 'Yes! But please, join us! I'd love to hear your adventure so far. No adventurer should be left behind, you know.'

'Annette!' Spirit yelled once again. 'He's a stranger!' I set Spirit into my bag again, hoping he'd stop when I did. Damien walked over and swiped a hand from the top of his head to his chin. Spirit fell under some loving trance as he echoed a purr. His smile said enough for me to continue. 'This isn't over though!'

I smiled back at Damien, 'You must be a good pet owner, Spirit is one stubborn cat sometimes.'

Damien had smiled back. We continued to walk across the meadow. 'I've studied the creatures around my neighbourhood for a while. Cats are always stubborn unless you know the tricks.'

'You need to teach me! Spirit is more stubborn than a boulder.' I laughed back.

We talked for a while, soon the sky became a gorgeous pink sunset. It was a shame we had to stop chatting, though we stopped in a small shadow area with few trees to set up camp. I flicked my wand out but Damien brought his hand up to stop me. 'Watch this.'

Damien held his wand out and readied himself. 'Ignis!' He confidently shouted. We watched the wood pieces carefully, trying to see a difference. I looked over at Damien, seeing him shake his wand again, 'Ignis!' He tried again. I stood curiously, why was he trying? Boys couldn't be witches I thought. 'Ignis!' Damien tried once more, his voice shaking in... nervousness?

'He's acting strange.' Spirit whispered to me. Damien looked at me, he heard what Spirit said.

'Here.' I went over and held my hands on top of his. I touch the wand to make sure my magic energy could come through. 'You need to concentrate on the wood pieces, imagine a flame coming out. Then, when your mind has captured a moment, you say the spell!' I readied myself.

Damien stopped and exhaled. 'Ignis!' He said confidently said once more. I transferred my magic to the makeshift jewel wand Damien held. I created the fire, in hopes he wouldn't notice. A beautiful fire swirled out of the wand's tip, searing the wood. I let go and kneeled down. I looked at Damien's stunned face. 'I did that?' His mouth hung open in astonishment but his eyes were lit up with hope and pride in his doing.

I didn't want to tell him that I had created the flame. Spirit chimed in instead. 'Annette did it.' I looked back at the black cat in anger. Why would he want to shatter his feelings? We just met him!

Damien exhaled, almost in dejection. 'Guess I'm still trying to get it right.' He shuffled a small chuckle under his breath. 'Not the best, not yet.'

'That's the mindset!' I joyously announced. 'Though, why are you practicing? I thought only girls can be witches.'

'I'm proving that wrong!' Damien smiled at me, in confidence and pride. 'My village sent me out to do some job but I'm practicing along the way. I wasn't making much progress until now.'

I smiled at his response. I had a warm feeling as Damien told his story. I was still confused, I've never heard of a boy witch before. I slid down a tree, feeling Spirit curl next to me in exhaust. 'What's the job?' I asked, hoping he'd continue his story.

There was no response as Damien had just settled down in a torn cape he wore. The realisation hit me, I have a new partner. A new companion to talk to, chat with, practice together. I hope he can break through and become a witch as well. We'd be the best partners in crime! The first boy witch, Damien! And me, the best witch to ever train! I felt my eyes grow heavier and soon fell asleep.

I woke up, feeling more tired than I had the previous days. I opened my eyes to the blinding sun hitting my face. The realisation had hit me, I woke up late! 'We're late!' I jumped up and swooped down to pick up my satchel. 'Spirit! Where are you? We're losing daylight!'

'Why are you in a hurry?' I heard a low voice call out to me. I looked towards a grey figure brightened by a fire. I rubbed my eyes to get rid of the sleepiness. The figure morphed into a boy about my size. He stood up, my eyes focused on his brightened wand in the holster.

Damien! I forgot he joined yesterday! We talked for hours as well! How could I forget? 'Damien! I slept a little longer than I usually do, sorry.'

The boy had chuckled. 'We aren't in any rush.' He guided me to the fire where he roasted some berries. Dried berries, Spirit and I usually ate whatever we found raw. 'Have some! Freshly roasted.'

Spirit had his small plate of dried berries on a plantain leaf. His muzzle was dyed blue from the berries. I chuckled until being served my own leaf of berries. 'Thank you!' I tried to start eating, though Spirit rushed in before me to eat my berries. 'Spirit!'

'These are way better than what you usually make!' Spirit laughed. Damien chuckled along, I glanced back at him and he instantly stopped. 'I left you some, eat up! I found something just up the hill.'

Another adventure? Great! I hurried my food and yanked Damien to start exploring, even if he wasn't done yet. 'Where?' I excitedly asked. Spirit shook his head but guided us anyways.

The three of us came out of the small forest and appeared to be next to a huge mountain range. Spirit trotted forward and we followed. I saw an oval shape with a scalloped pattern. The colours changed as we inched towards it. It started purple, then transformed into blue, then green. The light reflecting onto it must've changed it. 'What is it?'

'I've never seen one,' Spirit announced. I walked closer to it and Spirit followed. 'Damien, do you know?'

I looked at the grey kid to see his eyes widen but then he jolted his head away from the oval. 'I don't know! Maybe it's an egg!'

I gasped, 'What if it's a dragon egg?' I chuckled along with Spirit. It couldn't be a dragon egg. Only a handful have ever seen a dragon and told the tale, let alone seen a dragon egg. Dragons are so rare.

Damien's nervous laughter followed along with us. 'Maybe, we shouldn't be so close to it.' He went over and pulled me away from the egg. 'I'd hate for that to be true. Dragons are territorial creatures.'

'They are rare.' Spirit added, 'If this really is a dragon egg, why would it be at the bottom of the mountain?'

'I'm taking it!' I happily replied. I broke out of Damien's hold and picked up the possible egg. 'Whoa, it's pretty heavy.' Damien tried to take the egg away but I put the little oval into my bag. 'That's weird, it feels warm on my side.'

'Maybe we shouldn't take-' Damien started but perked his head up and closed his mouth. 'Alright, where are we off to next?'

Spirit's ears perked, 'Did one of you guys extinguish the fire?' I looked at Damien and he shook his head. Both of our eyes widened.

'The forest!' Damien yelled.

'The fresh roasted berries!' I yelled out. We both ran to our campsite and took care of the situation before it went out of control.

I happily skipped, knowing we now have a new partner and maybe a new baby creature. Even Spirit doesn't know what it could be! The idea of it hatching gave me the strength to trek forward! My mind couldn't decide on the creature that could hatch from it. Every now and then, my satchel shakes so I carry the egg.

'Put it away, Annette.' Spirit commanded, 'We can't risk it breaking.'

I sighed, 'It's shaking, is it cold?' I asked. Damien nervously smiled and lowered my arms back into my satchel. Does he understand egg language? What is he doing?

'It's cold! And being in the open air will make it even colder!' Damien nervously chuckled, put his head down and moved a little ahead of us. 'Definitely! Make sure it's safe and sound!'

I looked down at Spirit who looked at me with the same confused expression. I looked towards Damien,

'You've been acting awfully strange. You weren't this nervous when we first met.'

Damien slowed his stroll and turned back, 'I'm just realising about this adventure now! A new hatchling! Haha! We need to make sure the little dra-creature is perfectly safe when it does hatch.' He caught a mispronunciation in the middle of his sentence. It sounded as if it wasn't supposed to be as obvious as it did. 'I remember seeing a maikong Village on the next hill range, about a day's worth of walking.' Damien turned back and sighed in relief.

I shrugged my shoulders. 'Well, what should we name it? I was thinking Azalea!' I happily added.

'That sounds a little, unsuited for him,' Spirit argued.

'Him? What makes it a him? Azalea works for a genderless creature as well.'

'What if it's allergic to Azaleas?' Spirit argued again. 'Maybe he came from the high mountains and the meadow was foreign to his little hatchling self.'

'Well, smart one, what do you think?'

'How about we don't discuss a name!' Damien interrupted. He abruptly stopped in front of us, holding his arms out to stop us as well. 'I hear something.'

My bag moved again. I took out the egg and held it close to me. 'It's just the egg shivering again, it doesn't shake when it's in my arms.' I laid my cheek to the egg and I felt the warmth heat it up a little. 'I think it likes me, it warms up quite a bunch.'

'Shush!' Damien called at me. I looked down to see Spirit perk himself up. His ears twitched. A small rustle came from behind me. I cradled the egg in one arm as well as I could despite its size and reached for my wand in its holster. The rustle echoed in the forest around us. This wasn't just one thing.

'Fire!' A voice echoed from a distance. I saw arrows fly towards us as Damien grabbed my arm to flee. Some arrows were brightened by fire, some blended into the darkness. I looked around to see green people run at us, some ran at our pace to catch us off guard.

I dropped the egg into my satchel and reached for my broom. Spirit hopped onto my flowing cape. 'Grab the bag!' One man yelled out to his partner next to us. Why my bag? I dodged his lunge and jumped off the ground on my broom. Spirit climbed and entered my bag while I grabbed Damien's hand and hoisted him up.

'Are you insane? Flying on a broom through a forest!' Damien shouted. I yanked him up and he positioned himself on the bristled part.

'Yes!' I angled the broom to fly us through the treetops. We exited the branches with leaves around us. I could hear the echoes of the archers fleeting. 'We did it!'

Damien held me tightly on the broom, was he

scared of heights? 'Land us soon!'

I chuckled, it was somewhat adorable having him cling to me. I snapped my head out of the thoughts, flying us steadily until I felt exhausted. 'I thought you'd at least learn how to use a broom!'

'I'm trying to learn the basics first!' Damien yelled into my shoulder. 'Just land us soon! I can feel the bugs crawl over me already.'

I sighed, I can see a small village ahead of us. It was on the side of a mountain. That had to be the maikong Village Damien talked about. 'We'll land as soon as possible,' I reassured, heading directly to the village.

I landed in the central area of the village. Maikong people casually walked around us, chatting and having a stroll as though we hadn't just landed. 'Here!' I announced to the petrified Damien. He slowly lifted himself off the broom and crouched on the ground, reestablishing his strength.

Spirit hopped out of the satchel and onto the ground. I placed the broom back in my bag, though decided to hold it to avoid hurting the egg. 'Is this the maikong Village?' Spirit asked.

I had to help Damien stand up, he leaned on me as if his feet weren't working. 'No flying! No more.'

'Relax, we are in the village,' I reassured. 'They look so cool!'

'Visitors?' a feminine adult voice asked us. I turned to see a beautiful grey furred maikong standing before us. She wore a blue cloak and had a golden staff next to her. A jewel in the circle of the staff stayed perfectly still, though floated like it was attached to the ring! I found my mouth hanging open and quickly covered it. 'A witch, are you?'

She knows! My mind raced in excitement. 'Yes! I'm Annette and this is my companion, Spirit!' I looked back to see Damien on the floor again. 'That's my other friend, Damien! He doesn't particularly like flights.'

The maikong chuckled. 'You're an outgoing little girl. Come in, please! I just made some soup.' The maikong turned to walk into her homestead, I followed holding my satchel and broom.

I entered to see her home scattered with ingredients and herbs for potions. Vials lined shelves and spellbooks were carefully placed in several clusters. The homestead was smaller than I'd imagined, though I happily smiled at the colourful potions she had aligned. 'I smell vanilla!'

The cloaked lady chuckled at my comment, 'You should! It's my newest potion, the main ingredient of vanilla stands out.'

'You're a witch?' I asked. I should've already known from her house of vials and elegant staff. Though this made me realise who she really was. 'No! You're Miss

172

Circe! The best potion-making witch!'

'So you've heard!' Miss Circe smiled as she served a wooden bowl on a table. Her soup smelt as delightful as the vanilla. 'I'd say I exceeded a while ago. I left Ceat and saw my title diminished quite quickly,' she chuckled as she spooned some newly made soup into the bowl.

Spirit hopped onto the table. 'I beg to differ.' His voice caught Miss Circe's attention. 'Nice to see you again.'

'Spirit?' The witch turned around and started petting the cat. 'You're travelling with Spirit?'

'She's Annette, Madame Medea's heir,' Spirit announced. I felt myself blush. I knew my mum was famous, however I didn't expect this encounter.

'Medea had an heir?' Miss Circe bowed towards me. 'Such an honor to meet you.'

I smiled. 'Nice to meet you as well!' I bowed in return, assuming it was what you'd do when meeting another witch. Miss Circe chuckled as she served two more bowls of soup.

I saw Damien sit and relax at the table. 'Dear, you shouldn't be here.' Miss Circe announced as she served Damien his bowl and a wooden spoon to eat. 'Don't tell me he outcasted another one.'

Damien was abruptly set back but relaxed after seeing me. 'I don't think you have the right person.' At the end of his sentence, my bag started shaking again. I went to reach for it, however, Damien stopped me. 'Not now, Annette.'

'Why? It's shivering again?' I said.

Miss Circe sat herself down as well, 'It's shivering? What is it?'

I reached for my bag and pulled out the egg. 'We don't know what it is but it likes to be held!'

Miss Circe pushed herself back. 'Why would you have a dragon egg?' she yelled. My eyes widened and I backed away as well.

'Dragon?!' I got scared and dropped the egg on the table. Spirit jumped off the table and came beside me. 'I was holding a dragon this whole time?!'

The egg started rolling off the table but Damien caught it just in time. 'We can't hurt it! It needs to be in the best condition!'

'Did you know it was a D-r-a-g-o-n?' I asked. I figured we shouldn't yell out the word to avoid anyone outside hearing.

'Y-e-s! You don't need to spell it out, we all know it's a dragon egg now.' Damien mocked.

'Why didn't you tell us before? What were we going to do once it hatched then?'

'Hatch? Like now?' Spirit hopped back onto the table to see the egg viciously shake and start to crack. The egg started rolling around and Damien tried to stop it. Is it already about to hatch? What are we going to do? There is some angry dragon mum missing her baby! I don't want to be the one who shows the mum that I stole it! The tail of said dragon poked out of the eggshell, ruining the scalloped pattern. It was a blackened tail with red spikes.

My mind sprawled into a panic. The dragon mum is going to kill me! I'd hate to see what the mum would do! What about the dragon dad? 'What do we do?'

'Hold on!' Miss Circe turned and covered the egg with her fluffy tail. 'We need to make sure it won't roll away. I have some towels in the cabinet behind you Damien! I'll conjure a quick sleep potion so it won't attack.'

'Got it!' Damien fixed up some towels and placed them beside Miss Circe.

'Don't worry little buddy, we'll get you home soon!' I inched closer to the shell. A piece popped off to reveal a beady sharpened eye. 'It's still hatching, Miss Circe!'

'I see that Annette!' Miss Circe announced. 'There are a few leftover vanilla sticks in the vials, could you bring me some?'

I rushed over to pick one out. I came back to the shell being half opened. Spirit was pawing at the shell hoping to clean it up before putting on the potion. The legs and tail were exposed. I gave Miss Circe the stick and helped to move the top of the shell away. The dragon turned and stumbled towards me. It hobbled towards me with soaked wings. It rubbed it's head on my clean shirt, getting me messy in the process. 'I think it likes me!' I announced. Miss Circe made the potion and poured it into a small bowl. She saw me and stood in shock.

'Oh dear, the dragon likes you.' Miss Circe sighed in disbelief. 'It must've made an imprint on you first.'

'What does that mean?' I didn't know whether to smile or scream. The new addition is adorable but it's a dragon!

'It means, it thinks you are its mother.' Miss Circe said. She sprinkled the dusty potion around the dragon which knocked him unconscious, for now at least.

I took a step back. 'A dragon thinks I'm their mother.' I couldn't fully process what the situation was. 'What will we tell it? I don't want to tell it that I'm not the mother.' I felt a slap against the head to see Damien. 'What was that for?!'

Damien shook his head, 'It doesn't speak our language, obviously.' Damien looked at Miss Circe. 'What should we do?'

Miss Circe's eyes widened in shock and confusion. 'I don't know, I've never seen a dragon before. I've only read about it in books.' Miss Circe reached behind her and gave me a book on mythical creatures, The book of Mystical Encounters, the title said enough. Though, how would this tell me what to do next? I can't be a dragon mum. I'm barely a teenage witch!

Damien's hand slapped the table, 'Where can we deposit the dragon?' He demanded.

'Deposit? It's a dragon!' Spirit argued back.

'This is the richest opportunity!' Damien brightened at his idea. 'A dragon egg would've been too sketchy to turn in. Now a witch and a dragon!' A witch and a dragon? A richest opportunity? Was he planning to use me for money? I stood in disgust. I shuffled the dragon into my bag, making sure he could fit comfortably. He was indeed bigger than Spirit. 'Annette?' Damien looked at me with confusion, though his face sparked his realisation of what he had said.

My mind was frazzled with the idea, that's why his village sent him. He was travelling and found a witch, thus he would catch me and turn me in to get the benefits of golden coins. I felt convinced this was the case, though, I truly hoped it wasn't . 'What richest opportunity? To get two rare sights and prove to your village that you did your job?' I emphasized. I looked behind to see Damien shake in nervousness. 'What are you striving for, really?'

Damien opened to speak but Miss Circe chimed instead, 'I doubt that would be the case Annette, he has traveled alongside you and you two had become great friends. Why would he ruin his friendship in exchange for money?'

I questioned her credibility. She's just as vulnerable as the best potion-making witch. Though, I couldn't deny her thinking. I looked at Damien who looked down at my glance. I turned around to see that the sun had almost set down. Spirit rubbed against my leg and turned me to the table. 'Let's rest for tonight. We can figure everything else out in the morning.' Spirit reassured me. 'Miss Circe, mind if we stay the night?'

Miss Circe nodded, 'I believe I have one bed left in the guest room.' She gestured to the door in the back of her workshop.

I walked towards it, brushing past Damien as if I hadn't noticed him. 'That's all fine. There's only two of us.' I heard Damien exhale as he followed behind us.

I settled onto the bed, gently putting the new dragon next to me. My head switched from Damien to the new addition. Spirit settled a distance away from the dragon, though just enough to leave some space for me to lay down. I couldn't help but glance over at the boy on the ground. He covered himself with his torn greyish cape. 'You didn't mean it, right?' I asked as gently as I could, trying to fight the anger inside me. I waited for some movement, the room was pitch black, there were no candles lit up.

I heard a rustle. 'Not anymore.' Damien replied. I heard the sadness in his voice, though I couldn't decipher if he was sad because he lost his village's job or me… his friend.

'At first, you did then?' I asked. 'No,' I started a new question, 'you stated that you had a job, what was it?'

I heard no rustle. His voice broke the silence instead. 'To capture a witch.' I sat upright at the response. I was right, then. I wish I hadn't been right, though here we are. 'I travelled for some time looking for a witch. That day turned into weeks very slowly. Painfully slow. Then, I found you flying down on your broom.'

No, I gave myself away then. Damien continued anyways, 'You were nice, despite you threatening me at first. So I waited for the right moment and travelled with you. It was nice to have someone to talk to again.' I noticed my heart started beating a little faster. I was being swayed by his words. 'So, I was going to give up the job opportunity.'

I sighed in sorrow. My anger diminished into this sorrow. He changed his mind halfway through. I turned in the bed, trying to fall asleep. 'I'll apologize then.' I started, 'Sorry for accusing you about the capturing earlier. You changed and for the better.' I tried to calm my heartbeat, 'Sorry, truly.' I closed my eyes and eventually fell asleep.

I woke up facing the wall. I looked over to see a black

cat curled in a ball and Damien sleeping in his cape, facing towards me. I stretched before getting out of bed. I looked out of the carved window. The sun was shining, as if the world was at peace again.

Then, a scream caught me off guard. It sounded like it was from the kitchen. Miss Circe? I looked around, realising what was missing.

The dragon.

I rushed out of bed and flipped Spirit off the bed. 'Coming!' I yelled to the witch. I busted the door open to see Miss Circe training the tiny dragon with fire breathing. She held a dampened wooden spoon and the dragon would aim at it. It would shake its tail in the air then fire a flaming ball at the spoon. The fireball would dissipate once hitting the spoon, must've been a casted spell. 'Miss Circe?' I asked. I saw the witch turn to me while the dragon looked and ran to me, tripping over it's tail.

The dragon leaped off the table and flapped its tiny blackened wings. It almost fell to the floor but flew higher and crashed into me. I grabbed a hold of the dragon, sending me flying backwards. I felt two arms wrap around me, I looked up to see that Damien caught me. 'Thanks!' I regained my stability and stood up. 'Isn't it a bundle of joy?'

'He's a quick learner!' Miss Circe announced. 'He woke up and crawled to the kitchen quite early. I found him eating my leftover soup.'

We all laughed as I tried to contain the heavy dragon. Miss Circe said it was a him, so I'll take her word for it. It's like he grew a few inches while we slept! 'Well, I can't keep him.' I announced. I turned to Damien who nodded his head. 'The three of us need to get to Ceat. We're going to be the best witches out there.'

Miss Circe chuckled, 'I do believe this is a witch's problem to solve. You need to choose what you want to do.'

I looked in confusion. I couldn't leave the dragon with her? She enjoyed its company. Damien sighed for me, 'We need to return the dragon to his mother, right?' I stepped back, we can't!

'That's right.' I heard Spirit's voice come in. I stepped away from him as well. We can't go near the angered dragon mother! She'd kill us!

'You both aren't the least bit terrified?' I asked in shock. The two boys walked out of the door.

'Definitely scared.' Damien calmly said.

'Absolutely petrified.' Spirit chuckled. Was that sarcasm? I looked at Miss Circe, hoping she had a better idea.

'I wish you the best of luck.' Miss Circe smiled and bowed. I couldn't comprehend this experience. Mum never told me this could have happened! 'Oh and please take these!'

Miss Circe reached for three potion bottles of various bright colours and her dampened wooden spoon. 'The blue potion is a sleeping potion for if he gets upset. The green one is for Spirit if he gets hurt, it'll regenerate his wounds quickly. The purple potion was brewed for either you or Damien, to help your wounds.' The dragon got excited and started sniffing the bottles. Miss Circe placed them in a cloth and put them in my bag. 'You are going to be a great witch. Your mother would not have known what to do with a dragon.'

That sentence was the hope I needed. Miss Circe gave me a kiss on the forehead for luck and I nodded. 'Yes. Thank you! That's just what we needed!' I rushed out the doors with the dragon. 'Bye, Miss Circe!' I yelled back. I brought my broom out. The boys said their farewells and we all climbed onto the broom. I set Spirit into my satchel. The dragon flew beside my broom.

It's hard to believe, I set my mission to Ceat aside to help a baby dragon find his mother. Alongside a cat and a boy who tried to capture me, we will help a dragon. I smiled at that thought.

Mum would never believe me.

I'm quite possibly the best witch there is.

THE LOST HOME

by Danielle Adams

The cold cool air gently caressed the child's face. Each strand of hazel fur swayed as the air reached it. This time of year was not the dear child's favourite. Harsh winter weather was something she feared. Normally the cave that had become her home many years ago, would be the best shelter but that changed. The shaking maikong sat with her legs hanging off the edge of the rock. She was guarding a tomb. The tomb of her father. Now, this was not a custom within maikong tribes. Traditional burials were much more similar to practices within the Lupus race. This did not include tombs but decomposition in the ground. Unlike these strict traditions, this fox had created a new one. Although it most probably had something to do with who her father was. This young fox was not brought up by an elder maikong like most. She was found abandoned as a youngling and a mythical creature took her in. This creature was one of the many fabled dragons. A race thought to be dead. Vanished into nothing. No one knew if any still remained, they were thought to be lost to history. The young maikong was lucky to have known, possibly, the last dragon. However, he had now passed. His long secluded life had come to an end. It was not a sad death but one that was accepted as a peaceful goodbye. The dragon's child knew this day would come. She did not want to deal with it but it didn't come as a shock to her. Old age will take us all.

Moments had passed as the young fox sat watching the Zisu fly by. Their great wings caused hurricanes on the wrong day. Today, they flew in a formation as each white feather ruffled through the sky. It was somehow magical watching these birds perform. They were so elegant for such large creatures. Each curve in their glide seemed so simple, like a mundane task. But, to a small maikong, it seemed like a wish. Something that you would want to achieve but never could. As she wallowed in thought, the little fox began to rise from her seat. She leaned down to pick up her battered old bag and cloak. The velvet, emerald green cloak was flung around the fox, so that it lay evenly on both shoulders. She gently fastened the rusty pin that kept the cloth secure around her neck. The bag strap sat around the one shoulder, just hiding the warm cloak underneath. The bag was light brown, with a greyish tinge. There were many holes and places where the thread had loosened on the material. It was safe to say this bag had seen a great many adventures. Even the buckle keeping the bag shut had began to rust, to the point where you could not tell what the buckles original colour was. Once the maikong had adjusted herself, she slowly climbed down the mountain. Each footstep was carefully placed, making sure she never lost her footing.

Once back onto a stable footing, the young fox took a deep breath and stared at her surroundings. Lush rich forest land engulfed her view for miles. It seemed that her natural land was calling to her. The idea of a forest being a home was very foreign to the dear fox. To her, a cave full of cold and grimy calcium and water was the perfect home. I guess it all depends on our upbringing. She knew the forest land was where she was from. Her father had told her stories of it, told her all about her home. But it was not her home. Whilst considering these things, she still decided to press on and entered the bushes. While wandering, the fox saw every beautiful detail of the forest. Each majestic tree, with the brown, cracking bark that held intricate bright lime leaves. The sky could no longer be seen as the leaves created shelter. Each step the fox took left a trail of small imprints in the mud. Squelching and rustling was filling the silence, along with the faint chirping of birds. Everything seemed very calm and tranquil. The maikong was beginning to feel relaxed as she progressed further into the belly of the trees. Minutes began to merge into hours as the youngling explored every inch of the inner workings of this new land. She sniffed every tree and made sure to examine every rock. This was her playground and she intended to find every secret it was hiding. The further she progressed, the more she noticed strange markings on the trees. It appeared that various combinations of lines had been skillfully carved into the bark. Everywhere the youngling turned, more and more intricate carvings surfaced. As they were becoming more frequent, the fox trotted over to a fresh, luscious tree. Her matted fur traced the indent. The bark path trailed around in a simple circle. It seemed that the mark had been carved a long time ago. There were areas that had been chipped. Some areas had indications of water damage, where the bark had become darker in colour and started to rot. Everything seemed peaceful until the fox was brought out of her trance. Ears pricked up, her eyes widened as the crackling of branches began to get closer. She could tell the noise was prowling towards her. Her thoughts began to run wild. What danger lay near? Maybe this was her time? A light dampness gelled the fur surrounding her paws, as her breathing increased. It was coming closer. Almost here. Almost time. Her eyes shut in response to a louder crunch.

Limbs stiffened on her body as she gently turned around. The youngling felt overwhelmingly tense as she toyed with the idea of opening her eyes. Maybe she would die without having to witness the predator. Perhaps staying oblivious was for the best. However, nothing happened. Her lids slowly peeled apart to reveal an odd scene. A lizard stood on the floor next to her. It was looking back up at her with it's small purple eyes. A sigh of relief escaped the fox's mouth. Only a lizard, there was never anything to worry about. The youngling knelt down, making herself as level as she could with the creature. Slowly she petted it. With each stroke of her soft pad on the lizards scaly body, it snuggled closer towards it's affection giver. A sweet scene. The moment reminded the fox of the many times her dad would comfort her. She was such a cowardly child. There were many tears shed throughout her childhood and her father was always there to pick up the pieces. Her thoughts wondered to a day from that time.

Wind violently pushed the trees from left to right,

making each leaf join the vacuum of air pressure. As the wind fought against nature, the sun sent beams of warmth to compensate. The fox, then just a child, sat on the ledge next to a Zisu nest. The birds chirped and sang calling to their mothers. Each note increased in pitch as the wind picked up in pressure. It appeared they were distressed. Scared. Their pure feathers ruffled and betrayed their bodies. It was obvious they were finding it difficult to stay in their nests. Their great wings were wanting to fly, to take advantage of such a strong track. The small fox drew her attention back to the ledge. She inched backwards and clung onto the rock wall behind her. She had only left the safe cave to find some discarded twigs. While keeping balance, she gently stood up. As soon as she had, the mother Zisu landed onto the ledge. These birds were peaceful creatures luckily. So the fox had no worries about whether she would be eaten or not. Although, there was a new danger. The stone ledge started to crumble away. There was a great amount of force behind the Zisu's landing which was too much for the fragile rock. As the rock collapsed, it inched closer to where the fox was. She scrambled, trying her hardest to find something to hold onto, anything that she could use to climb up the rock wall. Her paws scraped against the wall as she struggled, finding nothing. The crumbling rock caught up with the young fox. She kept scrambling, until, she fell. The rock below her had completely collapsed. She was falling. Her body plummeted through the air. The only thing to break her fall was the forest below. She looked down to see the jagged edges of branches in the distance. The points getting closer and closer. A loud scream erupted from her mouth as terror washed over her body. Nausea started to well up inside her as she screamed to the point her stomach hurt. It wasn't long now. Soon she would be dead. She braced herself for the impact. For the inescapable doom but it never came. Instead she felt soft scales underneath her. There was no harsh pain as she had expected. No, only the softness. Almost as if she was on a body. Something alive. There was a warmth to the cushion of scales. Then, as she stayed still with her eyes still tight shut, she realised what she was on. Her father. She knew it was him. He had saved her.

Once her eyes had refocused on the scene before her, the youngling realised she was stroking the air. The little lizard had scuttled off. Her trance had left her unaware to the reality around her. She fell back and let her body glide onto the ground. All the fox could think about was her dad. Her eyes stared blankly at the tree branches above. They appeared like a shelter. Each branch weaving in and out, creating beautiful patterns. Every leaf sat proudly, showing themselves off as they created a blanket over the forest. It was something truly mesmerising to look at. Her mind wandered back to the memory that had played out right in front of her. That day. It was similar to today, I guess that's why she remembered it. A single tear trailed across the foxes face as she thought about all the happy memories with her father. All of the adventures they had. The many times he had told her stories from his past. Stories of the wars with the elves he had been in. Tales of creatures that had been lost in history. She missed every quirk he possessed. The small twitch his face did when she proved him wrong. But, overall she missed the company of someone who loved her. The parent to guide her through life. It would be a lie if she didn't feel let down. She did. She was not ready to go out in the world on her own. There was preparation needed that she never got. But, she knew that was not her father's fault. He was old and his time had come. There was nothing anyone could do. The fox wiped away her tears. She knew she needed to find a new family, a new home and that terrified her.

After sitting and thinking about her old life, the youngling pulled herself off of the uncomfortable forest floor and onto her feet. She looked around while knocking twigs and dirt off her fur. Slowly, her legs began to take her deeper into the forest. It was going to get dark soon, so she needed to find shelter. Who knew what evil lurked in these woods.

The forest amazed the fox. There was something new everywhere. Each corner of the forest was different but the biggest oddity was when the little one found a treehouse. She had never seen one before but she had heard stories. The maikong froze and stared at the structure. There was an old rope ladder on the trunk next to the fox. It led up to the house and connected to many more bridges higher up in the tree. The house itself looked very plain, it was a simple wood structure with two windows and a door that did not look too sturdy. However, vines and flowers decorated the window and it seemed that there was more inside. The fox grew more curious, so she gripped her soft paw onto the ladder and began to climb. The ladder swayed ever so slightly but it seemed to be secured to the trunk with vines. Once at the house, the fox peeked through the window but no one was there. Given this opportunity, she gave the door a small push and quickly scuttled in.

Inside the building was a small wooden table with a chair next to it. Some bowls sat on the table but there was nothing inside. On the other side of the house, there was a small bed with a cloth cover and what looked like feather pillows. As the maikong investigated the house, droplets of water started to patter outside. The window drew in all of the spitting and as it began to get heavier, the window began to dampen. There was nothing on the window to stop the rain, so the little fox took her bag off, placed it on the floor and curled up on the bed. She pulled the cloth around her for warmth and fell asleep to avoid the rain.

Warmth made the younglings fur feel like a knitted blanket. She stretched her legs and arms, extending each paw in the process. As she lay there, she could hear chatter from unknown voices and the clatter of metal. The chatter began to get closer and she opened her auburn eyes to see who was talking. Using her arms, she propped herself up and saw a creature that looked like herself. Their fur was a lighter colour brown but they had very similar eyes. They didn't seem to notice she had awoken, so the little fox stood up and walked closer to the stranger. The pads on her paws made a gentle pitter patter noise on the wooden floor. As she edged closer, the stranger looked directly at her, presumably the stranger had heard the younglings footsteps.

'Ah! You're awake, how are you feeling?' the stranger softly asked the youngling.

The little fox simply stared, trying to think about a response. She had learnt this language from her father but it was not her native tongue, so it always took her longer to respond.

'I am...okay, where am I?' She replied in a confused tone.

The stranger smiled at her warmly and took the maikongs paw. They walked through the rather large structure as the stranger explained the land she came from. The fox learnt that is was 'The High Wilds'. The hometown of the maikong. She was told about the history of these lands and given a grand tour of the central hub of the town. It was all a lot for the young fox to take in but she tried her best to understand and ask questions. It seemed the stranger was not an unfamiliar face. She had known the youngling before she had gone missing. She revealed the life the little foxes parents had lived, before moving on to the city, Fogvalor. The youngling listened and awed at the new home she had discovered. She had never expected to find her home when she left her father. No. She had only expected a small adventure where she would find a new place to live. She had never thought she would be brought back to her own kind. Let alone to find out about who she was born to be and what that meant.

SASKIA
by Kevin Peake

ONE

She was running out of time. She walked briskly but slowly making sure to avoid the bright sides of the city. Since she came to Ceat, the city for training witches, to learn how to become more powerful, she had been keeping a low profile. No one must know who she really was. Her sister didn't even know where she was. She knew she shouldn't be here but she was desperate. She had to learn more magical spells. With that, she would become more powerful and take back what was supposed to be hers.

Different thoughts roamed through her troubled mind as she made her way to her one room apartment. She had rented her own room immediately after she arrived, six months ago, instead of joining the other trainees in the provided dormitory. She didn't want to stay with anyone or even stay in a lodge. She loved her privacy. She made a stop at a junction watching as other witches made their way to their various covens. They all looked peaceful and happy. But she? She didn't even want to think about it.

When she got to her apartment, she summoned Melissa, her maid. 'Have you heard from Griff yet?'

'No, Princess Saskia,' Melissa replied, twisting her fingers nervously. 'I have been trying to reach him since you left but he is not responding.' Some witches had the ability to connect with others at any time, no matter where they might be. She was careful to explain herself properly. She didn't want to anger the princess. Saskia was compassionate but was also known to be of aggressive nature.

'Okay. You may leave now.' Saskia stood up from where she was sitting and stepped slowly to the window. She looked out of her window, wild trees and shrubs greeted her. This was one of the things she loved about the city. Natural vegetations everywhere. Colourful shrubs surrounding the city. Everything found in the city was awesome. The buildings were of very high architecture. The roads and pathways were so smooth, you could sleep on them. She was supposed to be enjoying the scenery but no. Things kept slipping from her fingers all the time. Maybe she was cursed by her parents before they died.' She had to admit that she wasn't a very good daughter but she loved them dearly and had a right to have what she wanted, at the right time.

Griff, the great elf, was immortal and an old friend from home. They had been friends even when her parents were still around. He was the only one she trusted after her sister. He had promised to get her information on what was happening in Lastra, the forbidden city. The city she had been trying to enter, without success, for the past year. To dethrone Eloise, the Queen mother who had snatched her beloved husband away from her with unseen forces that were beyond her. She did not understand why her husband was able to enter the city while she was left behind. So, it was great news when she heard Griff had succeeded in his journey to Lastra. With news from Griff, she was going to destroy Eloise and get her husband back. One way or the other. Nothing was going to stop her.

There was a sharp knock at the front door. Saskia was already in bed. Stretching her limbs lazily, she wondered who could be at the door at that time when she was having her beauty sleep. She loved her sleep so much. Her sister had often accused her of being too lazy to even raise a finger. She didn't deny it. What was there to do anyway? Nothing. With half closed eyes, she watched her maid walk towards the door, open it and invite the elf in. He stood at the door post towering over Melissa in all his glory. He had a huge cylindrical shape and was pure violet in colour. His colour was what Saskia loved about him, just like Lazar.

'At your service, my princess,' Griff said bowing slightly. He still held her in high esteem after all these years. That was a good sign. She sat up on her bed dragging the bed wrap along with her to cover her naked body.

'Thank you, Griff,' she said eyeing him up and down. 'What brings you here at this time?' She knew she was asking a stupid question.

'I have news, my princess.' He was still rooted on the spot, not moving a muscle or a limb and looking very stiff.

'Out with it, Griff. You know I'm not very patient,' she commanded.

'Eloise is expecting a child, my princess. When I heard the news, I decided to return at once,' he said the words slowly as if talking to a child. Saskia's hold of the bed wrap tightened.

'What do you mean?' Her voice was barely audible as if she was in pain. Griff stiffened more.

'The Queen mother is with Lazar's child.'

'No, it can't be.' All this time, she had believed that her husband was forced to get married to Eloise. But with this information, she couldn't tell anymore. What was she to do now?

'I'm sorry, my princess.'

'How did this happen? You were supposed to watch my Lazar for me!' she barked, her eyes focused on Griff. She couldn't believe this. Something was out of place.

'I have no idea, my princess. Forgive me,' he replied.

'Melissa!' Saskia turned her focus on the maid. She was sitting on one of the armchairs trying desperately to look calm. She didn't want to face Saskia's anger.

'Yes, princess Saskia.'

'Tell me. Did you know about this?' She knew Melissa had the gift of seeing the future. How could she not know about this beforehand? She felt like doing something bad at that moment but controlled herself. Casting a spell on her wouldn't solve anything now. This had to be resolved with clear minds.

'No, princess Saskia. I'm just hearing about it now. I didn't see anything.' She was trembling slightly, shifting from one foot to the other. The only power she had as a witch was that of seeing the future. Saskia could decide to destroy her right at this moment and she didn't want that. She was scared. What would happen now if Saskia did not believe her? She turned to the elf, silently pleading with her eyes to help her out.

The elf felt compassion towards her and said to Saskia. 'No one knows about this, my princess. Only your Lazar and Eloise. Even the royal household do not know about it yet. I only found out because they didn't know I was listening through the window.'

'That's okay, Griff. Thanks for coming back at such great haste.' She closed her eyes and took a slow breath to calm herself. 'But I need help. I need to go to Lastra after my training,' she added.

'Don't worry, my princess. I will be going back to Fogvalor immediately and I hope to find a way to help you,' he assured her.

'Thank you again, Griff. You have been so helpful.' She wiped at tears she didn't know were already flowing down her cheeks.

The elf turned to leave but stopped. Turning to her, he said. 'Maybe you could come home soon, my princess. I'm sure your sister misses you.'

'I miss Fogvalor too, Griff. But before I can think about going home, I need to finish what I came here for. Have a safe trip.' That brought an end to it and the elf hurriedly left.

TWO

The elf made his way through the vast vegetations that night. Saskia was a very good friend of his and the sister of the girl he loved. They had grown up together in Fogvalor. He knew Saskia was always persistent on getting what she wants. But still, he respected and liked her. She was fun to be around when they were younger and this issue at hand was making her desperate. He had kept some things about what was really happening in Lastra from her. He didn't want her to go mad with fury. When she got to Lastra, she would see things for herself but for now, that piece of information could wait. He had promised to help her and he would. Any way possible.

The journey was about ten days walk from Ceat but to him it could be done in a day. As an elf, he had the ability to walk very fast. He could cover a mile in five minutes without breaking a sweat and it didn't take him long to get to Fogvalor.

He met Eve, Saskia's sister sitting at his door post. Since Saskia left Fogvalor, Eve had been staying with him. As a friend at first and then as something more. They cherished each other's company dearly. But have not really proclaimed anything for each other. Griff didn't want to rush things, he preferred it slow and steady.

Eve was a very beautiful and powerful witch like her sister. But she was very calm and gentle unlike her more outgoing sister. He was surprised to see her outside. Had she sensed him coming and decided to wait up? He never fully understood these things. Her head was placed on her lap so she didn't notice as he walked up to her.

'Eve.' His voice was low. He didn't want to frighten her. She raised her head slowly towards the voice and a grin spread across her face. She leaped from the steps and into Griff's arms.

'I have missed you,' she proclaimed.

'Come on, my dear. It was just for two months,' he teased.

'Yes but I still missed you,' she insisted.

'Why are you sitting out here?' Griff asked gesturing around their surroundings. 'It's dangerous.'

'I know. I have been sitting here every night for some time now, just hoping you would come,' Eve said, lightly tugging on his shirt.

'So, you really did miss me?' Griff said chuckling.

'You know I did. Now, let's get inside.' She took his hand. 'I want to hear everything about your journey.'

She opened the door, dragged him inside and shut the door behind them, bolting it before stepping away from him. She took the lamp sitting on the centre table in the living room and lit all the other candles in the room. She went about to set a hot mug of green tea for him. She took a seat on the little green armchair and invited Griff to join her. He sat down with reluctance.

'I need to rest, Eve. We can talk tomorrow,' Griff said persuasively, sipping his tea with gusto. It had been so long.

'No, Griff. You said you would tell me everything when you get back. So, spill.'

'Yes and I'm back for good,' he said taking her hand in his and kissing it. He finished the tea and stood up to place the empty mug in the kitchen but Eve dragged him down.

'It's not fair,' she whined. In the end, he told her everything that happened excluding the real reason he went to Lastra or that he knew where her sister was. He had taken an oath set by Saskia not to reveal anything to anyone. At least, not before the mission was accomplished. He tossed and turned in bed that night, knowing he was deceiving the only woman he really cared about. But there was nothing he could do. It was either that or get destroyed by the princess.

***

A week later, the elf left his house at dawn leaving a note for Eve, telling her he was going to see a friend and would be back soon. He only hoped she wouldn't ask too many questions when he returned.

He made his way into the darkest parts of Fogvalor where most of the demonic elves inhabited. He wanted to meet with the most powerful one and find out ways to help Saskia out. It was a risky journey. Although they co-habited here in Fogvalor, they weren't very friendly. Only the royal family were allowed to marry anyone of their choice. But the rest all looked with scorn upon other races. He met with a group of drac's who each had different sizes and shaped horns, pointed tails and red eyes. The one he was going to see was very powerful and dangerous, or so he was told by those candid enough to show him directions.

He soon arrived at his destination which was a secluded shrine painted stark black and stunk of unthinkable potions that were scattered around the room. He resisted the urge to cover his nose with his hand as he entered the shrine. He sat down on a stool which was kept at the corner of the room and waited patiently to be attended to.

He looked around the room, taking note of potions of bizarre shapes and colours hanging from the thatched ceiling. There were a lot of covered bowls that probably contains potions for curing different ailments. He was there for almost ten minutes before a handsome looking demonic elf appeared before him. Griff was surprised because he was expecting him to look monstrous and mean. Noting his surprise, the demonic elf smiled.

'Call me Gary.' This surprised Griff even further. He stood up to acknowledge his presence.

'Thank you for seeing me. I'm Griff,' he said bowing in greeting.

'You are welcome, Griff.' He moved away from the door and sat down on a floor mat beside his potions. 'Tell me what you came for.'

'I want to know how to enter Lastra freely,' Griff replied getting straight to the point. He watched curiously as Gary spread some cowries on the floor.

'Huh. And who wants to have access to Lastra?' he asked staring at his cowries and not at him. He was curious. He didn't understand why anyone would want to go to Lastra. There was nothing worthwhile there.

'I'm sorry. But I'm under an oath. I can't give out any information about that,' Griff replied feeling his palms begin to sweat. What if he decides not to help him? Griff thought. The demonic elf kept his eyes on his cowries, muttering some inaudible incantations.

'Well, I will help you because its my job to do so,' he said, finally breaking the building tension. 'But it will cost you.'

'Thank you. I will pay any price,' Griff quickly assured him. Gary chuckled lightly making Griff suddenly conscious. He was so happy that the demonic elf agreed to help him, he didn't consider what the price could be.

'200 gnome gold pieces by night fall,' Gary told him.

'Thank you,' Griff replied with obvious relief. He was very happy with the way things were turning out. Everything was just working in his favour. The gnomes were a shorter race in Fogvalor. They possessed very dangerous magic and usually turned to stone in day light. They stayed underground. It was well known that the gnomes were a stingy breed. They had the golds and gems but never released it freely. A few years back, he had made friends with some gnomes in Fogvalor who loved to gamble at the darkest hour. He played along fine with them using his tricks and charms to win so many gold pieces. He had thousands of them hidden in an underground well in his house. No one knew about it. Not even Eve. They didn't make use of gold pieces for purchase. Silver pieces was the general currency acceptable in Fogvalor. So, this was the perfect opportunity to spend his golds.

'Please, tell me what I need,' he said.

'All you need is a dragon's egg and you would be able to travel to your hearts content,' Gary replied with ease. Griff's eyes sharpened slightly.

'A dragon's egg? But dragons are extinct.' This was unbelievable. How could this be?

'Yes, a dragon's egg. Dragons may or may not be extinct,' He said with mischief in his eyes. What was he not telling him? 'But there are eggs scattered around the world,' he explained.

'How will I be able to get these eggs if they are scattered around? How will I know where to find them?'

'Too many questions, Griff.' He gathered his cowries into a small bag by his side. ' I will get the dragon eggs for you.'

Griff clasped his hands in gratitude. 'Thank you very much.' He didn't even bother to ask how the demonic elf would get the eggs. It wasn't his business, he assumed.

'You will deliver the gold pieces to me tonight and I will deliver the dragon's eggs at your place in a weeks time,' he concluded.

'But why my place? I could come back here at the appointed time to collect them,' Griff suggested, thinking about how he was going to explain the presence of the great demonic elf at his house to Eve.

'No, that won't do. The eggs are very vulnerable and carrying it will attract a lot of attention from evil eyes.' He paused to look outside the shrine and continued. 'I will tell you more when I deliver the eggs to you. That's all for now. Good day.' He turned his back on Griff, signalling the end of the discussion and disappeared to where he came out from.

The demonic elf had to prepare for his journey to Waque, an elven city where dragon eggs were suspected to be. It was a three day journey. The city was a dangerous one. He only hoped the tales about the eggs were true. He didn't want to be disappointed. It was now left for Griff to make his way out of the shrine.

THREE

Saskia was late for her training as usual. She had never managed to get there on time because of over sleeping every day. The head witch, their teacher, frowned at her as she made her way to her spot on the floor. Although she was always late, she was a fast learner which was the reason the teacher never uttered a word of complaint about her lateness.

'Stand erect, guys. Straight posture!' the head witch commanded, totally ignoring her. They all responded promptly. They continued the series of tricks and spells outlined for that week with Saskia being the best as usual. The others looked at her with scorn. She gave them back the same look. What were they thinking? She wasn't here to compete with anyone. She had a great task ahead of her, getting into any issue with them would be a total waste of time and energy, so she ignored them. After the training, the head witch asked her to wait behind.

She sat on the floor and waited for her. She had not heard from the elf since he left and she was becoming bothered. She couldn't sleep at night because of too much thinking. She could have gone to Fogvalor to see what was going on. But doing that would involve meeting her sister and she didn't want that. She wanted to keep her sister out of her mission. Keep her safe. Things were not going as fast as she wanted. All her plans were crawling. She was already sick of the training too. She was almost like a teacher herself or even more.

'Madeline, I must commend you for your hard work,' said the head witch, taking a seat on the chair she had just brought in. Madeline was the name she gave them. She couldn't afford anyone getting to know exactly who she was.

'Thank you, Elissa. You are a good teacher,' she replied.

Turning her full attention on Saskia, the head witch said. 'I hear you are from Fogvalor.' Saskia's eyes widened. She stood up and dusted her body.

'How did you know about that? I never told anyone!' This was a shocker.

'The source is not important. You are from there, yes?' she asked again, narrowing her eyes.

'Yes, I am. That's where my home is,' she replied. Had someone been spying at her? She had been extremely careful with everything.

'Why are you here, Madeline? It seems you already know most of the things that I teach here. I have been watching you practice. Its like none other.' Elissa never minced words. She always got straight to the point. Saskia understood what she was silently asking. She wanted to know her family background. And that she could never divulge. If anyone knew she was from the royal family of Fogvalor, she would be sent back. In their world it was believed that the royal family were well endowed with enough powers and magic. There were fears that learning more magic would make them too powerful which could then make them turn against the whole world. But she wasn't here to destroy the world. She just wanted to help her husband. She felt a surge of anger but tampered it down. Not now.

'I'm here to learn, Elissa,' she simply said not looking at the head witch.

'I see. If you say so Madeline but if I feel you know too much, I would be forced to send you away. I need to create more space for the more immature witches out there,' she explained.

'That won't be a problem, Elissa. I will be going home soon.' She paused to stare at her fingers. 'Just a few more days.'

'Okay. You can go now. See you tomorrow,' Elissa said, dismissing her.

Saskia left the coven seething with anger. If only the elf had returned with help as promised, this wouldn't be happening. She had to prepare to leave Ceat immediately before Elissa found out anything more. She had even used a fake name to disguise herself but yet the head witch had discovered where she came from. What would she discover next? What she was doing was against their law and this was putting her at risk. She could be banished. She didn't care. Her plans were falling apart. She was falling apart. If she did not reach Griff today, she would go to Fogvalor. She was running out of time.

She entered her apartment that evening and met Griff sitting very comfortably on the sofa with a mug on his palm. Probably green tea, she thought.

'My princess,' the elf greeted immediately as his eyes landed on her.

'Griff,' she simply said. She had wanted to see him all week but now she was so tired. Ignoring him, she moved towards the drawer, searched for a change of clothes and went into the bathroom to change. Melissa, bless her, had drawn her a hot bath as usual. She quickly stripped and took a thorough bath sponging away invisible dirt from her hair and skin. Her hair was cut short so she didn't have any problem with drying it. She was out in no time, feeling refreshed and calm. She took a seat opposite Griff.

'Please, Melissa. Get me a mug of whatever the elf is having.'

'Yes, princess Saskia.'

'I'm sorry for keeping you waiting, Griff. I just needed to refresh myself.' She leaned back on the chair and inhaled deeply.

'No worries, my princess. I'm not in a hurry,' Griff replied softly.

'How is my sister?' These days she had been feeling unnecessary emotion and she didn't like it one bit. If she was to succeed, she would have to do away with emotions for now.

'She is in good hands,' he simply replied, taking a sip from his mug. Melissa arrived with a steaming mug and placed it on the centre table close to Saskia's reach.

'Here, princess Saskia.'

'Thanks, Melissa.' She took the mug and inhaled the richly scented tea. It felt like a balm to her being. Taking a sip, she turned her attention back to the elf.

'Tell me.' No more unnecessary words. Better to cut right to the point and get it over with.

'I have found a way, my princess.' Griff took another sip deliberately testing her patience. 'It's the dragon's egg. All you need to do is carry it in a small pouch around your waist. The eggs will act as a pathway to Lastra,' he explained. He watched as surprise, then relief played out on her face.

'I never knew there were still dragons,' she exclaimed.

'Neither did I. But here are.' He produced a black pouch of medium size and let her have a glimpse of the eggs. 'They are very vulnerable and can attract a lot of attention. No eyes must sense this on you, so you must not stay in a particular place for too long. I would recommend trekking,' he explained further. He wanted her to understand everything. Evil eyes could render the eggs ineffective. It had not been easy travelling with the eggs. His fast pace had helped him. Explaining to Eve why the demonic elf was at his place wasn't as difficult as he had thought. The demonic elf was known world wide as a great healer. He had easily told Eve he was sick and needed potions from him and that had solved it.

'Thanks, Griff. This means a lot to me,' she said, smiling broadly at him.

'You are always welcome, my princess,' he replied, returning her smile.

'But I hope you know you will be coming with me,' Saskia remarked fixing her gaze at some distance over his shoulder.

'Oh! I thought you were doing this alone,' he exclaimed, thinking about what he was going to tell Eve this time around. He exhaled sharply turning his face away.

'Don't worry about my sister. She can take care of herself. I'm sure she would understand when this is all over,' Saskia offered, reading his mind.

'Okay, my princess. But there is something you must know before we begin our journey.'

'I'm all ears, Griff. Spill.'

FOUR

How could Griff had kept such important information from her? How could Eloise have her husband under lock and chain when she was carrying his baby in her womb? She was insane. They were preparing to get on with their journey immediately. She was taking her maid with her too. Useful or useless, she needed as many heads as she could get and having them with her was good enough. Her husband was in danger and it was up to her to help him out in whatever way she could.

Griff had told her her husband was the Queen mother's prisoner. If this was true, then what was she planning? Kill her husband and use his blood as sacrifice? She had known Eloise long enough before she disappeared into Lastra and began her evil rule. She had heard a lot about her evil ways and magic practices. It was said that Lastra was a city for those lucky enough to find it. But what was lucky about serving under Eloise? It was a curse. And she didn't want her husband there. Her husband was an elf like Griff, an immortal, easily destructible. She had to get him out of there as soon as possible.

They had each tied their pouch containing dragon's eggs around their waist as requested, concealing it with their attires. Before they left, she asked Melissa about what would happen when they got to Lastra but the maid had claimed everything would be fine. Saskia felt she was keeping something from her. Whatever happened, she was prepared. She cleared out her few things from her apartment and they checked out. She had no intention of returning.

Exhausted from the tiring walk, Saskia asked the elf. 'Are you sure this is going to work? We have been on the move for more than a day now.' Griff who had been keeping his pace very slow to match the witches's slow steps was too tired for words. He pretended not to have heard her, silently picking at his nails.

'We will be there soon, princess Saskia,' Melissa answered with certainty.

'How do you know this, Melissa?' Saskia asked, her patience running thin.

With a shrug, she simply replied. 'I can feel something.'

'You better be right, Melissa or...' That was all she could get out before a great tornado swept them off their feet, taking them to the unknown. After a torturous experience caused by swaying round and round, they landed on solid ground. They were breathing heavily. Saskia was holding her stomach which she had landed on. The others weren't better off.

'Phew! That was a first,' Saskia commented, dusting

dirt from her body.

'We are here,' Griff confirmed. He looked around them with relief. Nothing had changed. This was the exact place he had landed when he was transported here some months ago. The city was very beautiful. All of the houses were decorated with abundant sparkling gems of different colours. He assumed that this was the reason most of them stayed behind and never left. It was a beautiful place.

'Good. Lead the way,' Saskia said. She didn't even notice the sparkling houses. She didn't care about that. This city was holding Lazar captive and she didn't like it at all. There was no time to waste. They had landed on a vast clearing surrounded by short shrubs, so no one noticed them immediately. The elf led the way, moving towards the direction of the buildings. They passed others going about their business. No one paid them any attention.

Griff made an abrupt stop when they got to a secluded barn behind a vast building. Saskia assumed it was the royal house.

'Here is the palace?' she asked quietly, pointing at the building.

'Yes it is,'Griff replied, scoring their surrounding with agitation. 'Now, we have to figure out a way to get in.'

They disguised themselves with the colours they had brought along with them by covering their faces with it. When they got to the front of the royal house, they were met with a great crowd. There were others waiting to be allowed into the palace to pay homage to the Queen mother. Homage my foot! Saskia thought darkly. She couldn't wait to get her claws on the so-called Queen mother. As the palace guards ushered the crowd into the palace, Saskia and her team joined them. Sneaking into the royal house was easy enough. With the help of Griff, they were able to locate the royal room in no time. Saskia sent Griff and Melissa to go in search of Lazar while she dealt with Eloise.

'Is the Queen mother in?' she asked the elf at the door. When he looked at her suspiciously, she added. 'I want to pay homage to her.'

'Yes, the Queen mother is in,' the guard replied. This was perfect. She gestured to him to open the door for her and he did without question. She walked in and the door was shut behind her.

There she was. Sitting comfortably on her royal throne. Clutching her hand fan and looking very serene like everything was so good. She was looking towards the window, probably watching those outside and didn't notice as Saskia walked towards her until she spoke up.

'Queen Eliose.' The Queen mother flinched, turning her gaze away from the window. Was she too used to being called Queen mother? Well, Saskia couldn't care less. She wasn't one of her people. Too bad.

She sharpened her gaze on Saskia. 'Who are you?'

'I am Saskia,' Saskia replied with a smirk on her face. This was going smoothly.

'What do you want?' she asked, suddenly looking uncomfortable. Did she know who she was? Saskia thought.

'I am here to take my husband home, if you don't mind,' she replied sweetly. She was trying to irritate her and it was working. Eloise looked away.

'Who is your husband?'

'Oh! So, you have a lot of them locked up.' It wasn't a question. Eloise ignored her.

'I want my Lazar back. I know he is here,' she said calmly but was boiling with anger. Eloise was acting unconcerned and feigning innocence.

'Is that so?' She turned her attention back to Saskia. 'Lazar is the father of my baby. We are married now. Didn't you know that?' She smiled broadly.

'What?!' Saskia barked. 'How could you have the father of your child in prison? Are you insane?' She balled her fists. Eloise was out of her mind.

'Release my husband now!'

'And if I don't?' She stood up from her throne. She was so tall. That took Saskia aback for a moment. 'What would you...' Saskia did not allow her to finish.

With Saskia's eyes raging with hatred, Eloise was raised from her feet and thrown into the wall. Eloise stood up quickly, looking shocked. She hadn't been expecting that. She conjured up her own spells and threw Saskia to the other side.

'You are too weak, Saskia.' She walked towards her, staring down at her with disdain. Pretending to have lost consciousness, Saskia waited. 'This child I'm carrying is going to be very powerful. And with him, I will conquer the whole world. You could have joined me but no. I have no use of you.' She laughed loudly, spurring Saskia into action. She opened her eyes in time to see Eloise produce some bluish powder wrapped in a paper bag.

'I am going to destroy you once and for all, Saskia.' Saskia jumped up, catching her by surprise. The powder dropped from her hands spilling all over her legs. Saskia stepped back. She watched in horror as the powder started eating away at Eloise's legs, moving gradually upwards.

'No!' Eloise screamed. 'No!' She fell down screaming and cursing at Saskia. The powder disintegrated her whole body leaving only bluish ashes behind. Saskia was shaking. She never knew such dark magic existed. All she had planned was to fight Eloise until she was too weak to fight back, destroy her and then escape with her husband. This was too easy. She had wanted to show Eloise what she was capable of but it was obvious Eloise had wanted to end the fight quickly to avoid defeat which back fired.

Saskia quickly left the room, smiling brightly at the stupid guard when the door was opened, as if everything was fine and then she disappeared in search of her team. If they were successful, they had planned to meet at the back of the barn. Saskia hoped that they were as successful as she was. When she got there, she met only Melissa and Lazar. She went straight into Lazars outstretched arms.

'I'm so happy to see you,' she said, hugging him tightly. His arms were full of dark bruises and injuries but that didn't matter. He was alive and well.

'Me too, my dear,' Lazar replied. He looked so handsome, even with the dark bruises all over his face. He was just like Griff. Yes, Griff. She thought. Where was he?

'Where is Griff?' Saskia asked, looking around the barn.

'I'm sorry, princess Saskia. But he didn't make it. One of the guards put a blade in his chest,' Melissa answered, fresh tears pooling in her eyes. She was clutching a piece of his garment. In her excitement of seeing Lazar, she hadn't noticed that Melissa was crying. Saskia's face fell. This hadn't been entirely successful. What was she going to tell her sister?

FIVE

They made their way back to Fogvalor that same day. Arriving after two days of a hectic journey. They went straight to the royal house. Expecting to meet her sister, Saskia was disappointed. The house looked abandoned. When her parents were destroyed, she had dismissed all the maids and servants. Except Melissa. Her parents had died at the hands of one of the maids through food poisoning. She had watched the life sucked out from them. It wasn't a good memory and she suddenly felt lonely. She needed her sister. Telling Lazar to feel at home and instructing Melissa to make a home remedy for his injuries, she left in haste to look for her sister. Only one place came to mind. She had always known her sister loved the elf, even though Eve had kept it from her. It was a good thing they could marry anyone of their choice and now Griff was gone. She felt guilty. She had caused his death. If she hadn't involved him from the beginning, this wouldn't have happened.

She met her sitting on his front steps staring into space. Before she realised Eve had seen her, she was already hugging her.

'I have missed you so much, Saskia.' She was weeping with joy.

'I'm sorry. I missed you too,' Saskia replied, hugging

her tightly. This was what she wanted. A hug from someone who understood her perfectly. They stayed that way for some minutes before they finally released each other.

'Come in.' Eve invited her into the cozy room. 'Have you heard from Griff?' she asked when they were both seated. And then Saskia began her confession.

GOLDEN SEWER
by Alex Stabler

Once, far above the High Wilds, the elven settlements of Silane and Waque and the forest of the Wisu, which was said to be home to dragons, there was an island. The Slay Waterways was the home of the demonic elves known as the drac race. It's water was teeming with snarks. Small but vicious creatures with big, black teeth. Above the Slay Waterways was an island which steered a separate course through the sky. The gnomes of Kai Darl mined their treasures oblivious to its course. The witches who trained at Ceat, the purveyors of magical knowledge, had long forgot its existence, as did the lepus' of Tuskbane. Even in Fogvalor, a mutual haven for all races, did they forget this once-mighty island named Lastra. Nonetheless, high above the clouds, this slab of rock still sailed through the skies, though control of its direction was lost long ago.

The city of Lastra was divided into five districts for each of the species who lived there, each mirroring the culture of the particular species. Each was equally proportioned, except the Elven District, which was twice as large to make way for the two varieties of elf. Gnomes, lepus' and the maikong each boasted their own district, all circling the Dragon District in the middle of the city.

The Grand Palace, situated in the centre of the Dragon District, was built as a beacon of solidarity between the races all those years ago. The world had not always been so peaceful and for many, this was a crucial step towards peace under one rule.

Deep inside the palace, one door to the right of the throne room, was a dusty, round table. Plaques at each of the places were marked with the names of the leaders of each of the six races' factions. Six skeletons, motionless, sat at the last meeting of the round table, rotten food long forgotten, churning on their plates.

At the head of the table, the chair was left empty. The ghost of its owner was only denoted by a plaque. The same plaque tarnished the throne next door – 'Ravynne' – though in the room next door she was given the title of 'Empress'.

It was once again time for Empress Ravynne to greet

her subjects. This was always her favourite time of the day – she never missed it, not once – but she had to be prepared. She had to keep up appearances and today was more important than usual; for her, it was a crucial step towards peace, finally, under one rule.

She adjusted her gown and slipped her crown back onto her head – she despised taking it off for too long – tucking her ears underneath it. They wouldn't dare call her a bunny again – not when they can't see them, or her tail. She narrowed her eyes – ugh, how often she wished she'd been born any species other than lepus. But her hair looked wrong without the ears either side; she adjusted her hair again and again and, no, one more time. Was that a wrinkle? Oh, no, of course not. Never. Finally, she was ready. Just as well – Empress Ravynne was never late.

A large crowd was waiting in the Palace Square, right in the middle of the Dragon District, where all the districts met.

As the Empress walked down the steps of the Grand Palace with a legion of guards surrounding her, the crowd stirred in anticipation.

'All hail the Empress!' one of the many guards shouted.

'All hail the Empress!' the crowd volleyed.

Quite right, the Empress thought. They knew their place. The sooner this rebellion nonsense was dealt with, the better.

She turned her attention to the matter at hand: Arigim Quorick was locked inside a darkened box – a tiny slit of light slicing its way through onto his skin. She looked through the tiny gap, looking him over for a second. He wouldn't be missed by many, surely.

She turned to face the crowd of equally dirty faces. 'This man, Ogrim Brandmar – a gnome of all things – has been judged guilty of conspiring against Lastra and its Empress.' The crowd restlessly awaited the next words. 'For that, the punishment is clear.'

She nodded to one of the guards, who walked over and began turning a winch on the side of the box. Slowly, the top of the box came apart – split into two pieces – and light poured into the box.

The light burned his skin and he wriggled in searing agony as his feet, then his arms, his chest, his hands, his legs, his neck, his ears, all solidified into stone. His eyes blinked his last tear, forever preserved as it set.

'Let this serve as a lesson to you all,' the Empress called out to her subjects. She scanned the crowd and found her prize – at the back, in the shade: Isobys Quorick, the accused's sister. Their eyes met. 'A similar fate waits for any citizen who rebels against your Empress.'

And then she walked back inside. The crowd dissipated but Isobys stayed where she was. The

Empress' icy words freezing her in place, her eyes wide with fear.

Does she know?

Not too many houses and streets away, a similarly large crowd of Lastrians was forming but none of the faces seen at the Empress's gathering would dare show here. No, this was an altogether more secret affair – and the crowd was getting restless. The Empress and her bodyguards would only be preoccupied for so long.

At this end of the Dragon District was a long-disused stage, the venue for tonight's event. Once, this was at the forefront of a technologically marvellous city, a tourist destination for millions all across the world to visit. Music, theatre, speeches; all manners of entertainment would have been the spectacle here – that was the plan anyway. Nobody could quite remember how Empress Ravynne seized power but they knew things were never quite the same again.

Isobys sprinted in and just in time. She kept just to the edge of the shade; the sun was setting but was still as bright as ever. The merciful cover of night couldn't come fast enough. Where others slept, hiding themselves away from its terrors, that black backdrop was the gnomes' playground – or at least Isobys'.

She had been the perfect choice all those months ago.

Isobys' eyes darted towards Zis – Zissibyf Nelati, in full, though nobody called her that. She was a lepus, like the Empress, though unlike her in every other way; she was late and her fur glistened with sweat as she sprinted towards the stage. If anyone dared call her 'elegant' or 'beautiful' she'd respond in the most violent way possible.

It wasn't long until the crowd noticed her arrival either. She was the reason they were there. They settled down and for a moment there was nothing but silence. It felt like the entire city was waiting on one woman to speak.

She walked up to the stage and cleared her throat, gathering her thoughts. 'I won't ask you to kneel before me. I won't ask you to swear allegiance. I won't punish betrayal – I'd be disappointed if you caved to fear but I'd understand.'

She eyed Isobys, who knew too well what she was talking about: her dear brother. Whether loyal to the Empress or the rebellion, he was a traitor to most.

Zis allowed the silence to resonate. 'That said, I implore you, as a fellow citizen of Lastra, to stand by my side. Not with me as your leader, no – I would never stand for such a thing – but as comrades.' Most of the crowd nodded in agreement. 'Thank you. There will be a signal. I fear I would say too much to reveal my plans but you'll know what it is when you see it.'

She looked around awkwardly. There were so many things to say but so little time. This would have to do. 'Time is short, my friends. All will be well soon but the wheels are in motion. I fear for all our lives if I drag this out too long.'

She paused for a second, contemplating. Dare she say the forbidden words?

Yes. 'May the Life Giver bless you always,' she said and she walked down the steps.

The crowd followed her as she wiped the nervous sweat from her brow, they then started to go their separate ways. Isobys couldn't help but wonder if they respected her a little too much.

Zis grabbed Isobys' arm and eased her back into the shade. 'Easy there.'

'It's okay. It's safe.'

'I know, I know. But I worry about you.'

Isobys smiled and blushed. 'Please don't,' she said, avoiding Zis' eye. 'The Gnome District is shaded. I'm fine.'

'Okay. Is there somewhere we can talk? We have to act tonight.'

'Um…' she scratched her chin, searching her mental maps for a discreet location. 'Yes, there is a place. Follow me.'

Zis creased the corner of her mouth into a cheeky smile. 'Lead the way.'

Golden Sewer by Alex Stabler

It was in the darkest alleyway of the darkest district of Lastra that their plans were laid. Come night, they would break in to the Grand Lastran Library; once, the greatest library in the world, much of its knowledge was sealed off after the rise of Empress Ravynne. Beyond the doors which were sealed off centuries ago, there were corridors and corridors of forbidden books.

'But what could we hope to find in there, beyond books and dust?' Isobys asked.

'Knowledge,' Zis replied. 'Knowledge! From before. If we hope to restore Lastra to its glory days – or, rather, to restore it to its original vision – we have to find out what it is.'

To enter the library, the services of a handsome thief had been procured for an even handsomer fee. Ivran Oriro, a demonic elf, was a high-profile figure in Lastra. An advisor to Empress Ravynne herself and her delegate on matters of crime and finance. He was a risky man to approach but it paid off. They'd crossed paths before and Zis was impressed by his skills. He'd once been loyal but he'd become disillusioned by the Empress' rule.

'He's been stealing from the Empress right under her nose for years and she hasn't batted an eyelid,' Isobys said, almost impressed.

'Well, in his words…' Zis said, 'It's so much harder

to believe someone is a thief when they've already proven to not be one.'

But proof, he said, can be faked; with his skills, he was able to clear the area of the Dragon District around the library for just enough time to slip inside.

Once inside, what must be done would become clear.

'How can you be sure he won't rat us out?' Isobys asked.

'Don't worry. I've seen to that,' Zis replied.

'The lock is simple and ancient,' Ivran said. 'Well, for me, anyway!' He flashed a smile, then turned back to the job at hand. 'We will be inside in no time.'

Zis and Isobys exchanged glances, their unamused expressions dimly lit by the moon. Isobys looked down at the ground, noticing perhaps for the first time how much nicer the paving stones looked under the lunar light.

With a satisfying clank the door was unlocked. It swung open, revealing an unlit, pitch black room so different from the library most knew. They crept inside, keeping to the edges of the corridors, holding on to the bookcases – they dared not light the candles.

This was Isobys' first time in the library – what with it being closed at night – and it was everything she expected it would be and more. The Gnome District had its own library, as did all the districts – containing literature tailored to their specific cultures – but this was something else. Even in the dark, the staircases spiralling upwards as far as the eye could see, taking any who cared to wander along shelves and shelves and shelves and shelves of knowledge just waiting to be read.

'It's magnificent,' Isobys said, as a huge grin rose from her mouth to her eyes in a flash.

'Isn't it just?' replied Zis, returning her grin. 'Come on, this way.' She grabbed Isobys' hand and led her up one of the many staircases.

'You don't need to hold my hand, you know. I'm not afraid of the dark.'

'I know,' she said. She turned back, revealing the tiniest glint of a smile through the darkness.

Zis couldn't see the smile Isobys returned but she felt her hand grip tighter and that was enough.

Ivran followed them as they swiftly made their way up and through the library's corridors. 'Never been too fond of the dark, myself,' he admitted. 'Only adds to the disguise, I suppose.'

After all, who would suspect a coward of being a hero?

Eventually, on the second floor, they reached the secret entrance to the forbidden section.

'How do you know about this?' Isobys asked.

Ivran paused. 'It wasn't easy to find,' he said. 'I had to dig through piles of files – discreetly, of course. And the Empress purged most of the files from before her rule. Thankfully, not everything was destroyed. People's diaries, for instance. And eventually, I found what I needed to know.'

'Which was?' Zis asked.

'That there's a switch... a button, I think... somewhere around here...' He reached around the back of a bookcase, feeling around. 'Come on....' Nothing. 'Come on! It was... it was right here. That's what the diary said. To the left of the... yeah...' He looked around the room, getting his bearings.

'We trust you,' Isobys said. 'Take a deep breath.'

'I'll get a candle, if that helps?' Zis suggested. 'There are no windows up here, so we'll be fine I think.'

He nodded, burying his head in his hands. He was sure he'd been right.

Zis returned with the candle and pointed it behind the bookcase. They peered behind it.

'Ah! There!' Isobys cried. There was a small hole in the back of the bookcase and the remnants of something left behind. 'Looks like something's been sawn off.'

'Yes!' said Ivran. 'There was a switch here but it's been removed. But the mechanism must still be functional…' He thought for a second.

'Is there a way we can activate it?' asked Zis.

He nodded. 'Yes, I think so. If we can just replicate the…' His eyes widened as the tiniest spark of an idea fired his mind into action. He emptied the bookcase of its contents and flipped it forwards a little, gesturing for Zis to give him the candle.

He grinned, pouring hot wax into the hole. 'The mechanism is still working, I think. It's just the button that's missing. So… with luck… this should activate it.'

Sure enough, once the books had been placed back in the bookshelf and they'd given the wax time to dry, the bookcase swivelled around and they found themselves standing at the entrance to a forgotten world.

It was the largest treasure trove of books you would ever set your eyes on. They didn't have time to light all the candles but even in the dark it was beautiful; a glimmer of moon-light slid through a glass roof, giving just enough light.

The place had been sealed off for so long but it was all in such pristine condition. Zis had no idea where to begin looking but the information would certainly be there somewhere.

Isobys wandered the endless corridors of books and grabbed the first book that caught her eye. Crimson red, it looked freshly bound. She opened it and read the words.

'Dark clouds gathered overhead on the morning she came.' Strange, she thought. Aren't clouds below Lastra? She knew nothing but a clear sky above her head and here this book was describing the opposite. She turned to another page: 'The city came over the island of Ceat and as the morning sun rose I could just make out their new recruits making their way inside.' What was this strange place this book spoke of? 'Ceat' – how's that pronounced? 'See-at'? 'Kee-at'? 'Keet'?

Elsewhere, Ivran had uncovered another pristine old tome: 'The Origins of Lastra' was written in neat handwriting on its cover. He flicked through its pages – scanning the text for useful information. Floating city, airships, Cideolarth? What's tha – then he stopped and stared at a name which caught his eye.

Under a list of names 'The First Elected Council of Lastra' was 'Ravynne, Representative of the Lepus District.' She was on the council? No, that can't be right. She'd told him herself that the entire council had 'disappeared' – and implied worse. Clearly, there was more to this story.

Finally, Zis had found what she was looking for: city plans. She'd hoped to find something like this – she'd even brought a map of the city in the present day to compare it with.

Wow, she thought, not for the first time that visit. It

had it all. It was to be a paradise floating in the skies, with so much more to marvel at than the never-used stage she spoke on earlier. A sports stadium, public baths, museums detailing the history of the entire world, the finest restaurants, theatres, airship factory and station and more; Lastra was to be the marvel of the world and now she had no idea what the world even looked like.

With the information collected, they met up. 'I've found original city plans. We can definitely use these.' Zis said. 'Anything else?'

'I've started to unravel some of Ravynne's lies,' said Ivran. 'She was a member of the council.'

'Interesting. We'll have to ask her about that. And… and you, Isobys? What did you find?'

'Well…' she stuttered. 'It's not much but…'

Zis approached her. 'Go on.'

'Clouds. It's… the clouds. They used to be above us.'

She didn't know what to say. 'Above us? Are you sure?'

'Clouds. Yeah, they used to be in the sky, not… the sea.'

'Or…' Ivran chipped in, 'perhaps they were always in the same place and Lastra used to be below them?'

'We floated upwards! Yes!' Zis paced around, thinking furiously. 'We're a floating island. Something could have gone wrong.' She walked over to Isobys again and put her hand on her shoulder. 'This is good. You did well.'

She looked into her eyes. 'Thank you.'

Ivran looked at the two of them together and smiled to himself.

They scoured the library for hours, searching for explanations to the questions they'd dug up. Isobys and Ivran read and re-read their books and searched for more, while Zis looked over her maps.

Eventually, she ran towards them, clutching her maps. She'd found something.

She cleared a table and put them down side by side. 'Look at the buildings that have been built. The ones that weren't scrapped.'

'They're all the same,' said Isobys.

'Most of them,' she replied. 'Look at all of them, one by one. The Grand Palace, the Stage, even the Drunk Maikong. They're all picture-perfect recreations from one map to the other, apart from one thing.'

Ivran eventually chipped in. 'The sewers.'

'Yes!' she cried, a little too loud. 'Exactly!' She turned to Isobys, a huge grin on her face.

But she had no idea what she was talking about. 'What do you mean?' Isobys said.

'They're made of gold.' she answered. 'In the first, they're made of stone. But today, the sewers underneath the Grand Palace, they're made of gold. Why would they be made of gold?'

'Symbol of wealth, perhaps?' suggested Ivran.

'No,' Isobsys said, a little too quickly. 'Sorry, I just… Okay, this might sound weird.'

'No, go on,' Zis reassured. 'What is it?'

'Dragons,' she said. 'Dragons are afraid of gold.' Her face and hands alike shook with the realisation of the significance of this. 'That's what all the stories say anyway.'

'My word,' said Ivran. 'Cideolarth…'

'What?' Zis asked.

'The Life Giver.'

Ivran led them to the history book he had been perusing. 'This book describes a certain 'Cideolarth' – in the dragon tongue 'The Life Giver' – as being pivotal to the livelihood of Lastra,' he told Zis and Isobys.

Then he sat down. 'My word. We have stories in the Eleven District about the Life Giver… Cideolarth… but I never for one second thought they'd be true.'

'What stories?' Isobys asked. 'I know the phrase – the forbidden phrase – Zis used: 'May the Life Giver bless you always'. But that's about it.'

'The source of life, a mighty dragon who carries the world on his back. Even the elements bend to his will. Some even say he's who the council served. But I thought they were just stories… I don't know if they're all true but the root, the subject of the stories seems to be.'

'And with the sewers being made of gold…' Zis thought aloud, 'I'd say there's a decent chance Ravynne has him locked up down there.'

There was only one way to find out. It was a long and hard climb around the edge of the floating island, using makeshift pickaxes to climb up into the sewer system, which dropped out into the cloud ocean but thankfully it was an uneventful one.

Isobys and Zis pulled themselves up into the sewers just as the sun began to rise. They looked over the clouds, wondering what might lie beneath them. Maybe soon they would find out.

But it was promising. Zis tapped the side of the sewer. 'Gold. And this is the only exit to the outside.'

'So, if we follow this, we'll find the dragon?'

'Cideolarth, yeah. Here's hoping.' Zis grabbed her hand and led the way.

'Ivran was helpful in the library,' Isobys said. They'd left him in the city – his job was to distract Ravynne until the time was right.

'Yeah. He'll have his uses later as well,' she smirked at Isobys.

'Why are you so mysterious?' she responded. 'The

same reason I couldn't tell the public last night. Who knows how many ears these walls might have. And besides, the plan might not work if I tell everyone.'

'Come on, Zis,' Isobys said. 'I'm not just everyone. Even Ivran could see that.'

'No, no you're not. Which makes it harder, Isobys… Issy.'

Isobys smiled to herself. Issy… she liked that.

Zis stopped and turned to her. 'I need you to trust me.'

'Okay.' She nodded. 'Okay, I trust you.'

It wasn't long until they came across a gate.

Isobys tried it – locked. She sighed. 'If only Ivran were here.'

'He'd only get jealous. Come on, we can do it together. After three.'

Drip. A bead of water slipped down from the ceiling onto the floor.

'One!' Zis said.

Drip. Another one. Louder this time.

'Two!'

Drip, drip, drip.

'Three!' Together, they smashed against the gate. It didn't move.

Drip, drip, drip, drip.

Isobys looked down to her feet to see the water level

rising. Impossible.

Then it started raining down harder. Impossible drips sped down from the ceiling, spattering them and flooding the sewers faster than they could imagine possible.

'Quickly! After two!' Zis shouted. 'One! Two!' They smashed against the gate but it still wouldn't open.

A wet arm lashed out from the rising water, almost at one with the liquid itself. They flinched, their movements splashing the water against themselves.

'Again!' Zis said. 'One! Two!' Still no luck.

The water level rose further still, a face emerging from the depths. 'Who dares trespass here?' a whispering voice said.

Zis spoke, her voice trembling. 'My name is Zissibyf Nelati. Zis for short. And this is Issy – Isobys.'

'Isobys Quorick.'

No reply. The torrent fell from the ceiling faster still. The water was seeping upwards, masking their waists, chests and necks. Isobys took one last look at Zis before closing her eyes.

But Zis wasn't looking. She stared forwards, ignoring the water, channelling the strength needed for the both of them. She spoke softly: 'We're here to free the dragon.'

The water stopped dripping and slowly seeped through the floor. Then the gate swung open.

Isobys opened her eyes, surprised and looked to Zis. 'What was that?'

'No idea. At a guess… magical defence.'

'So we're heading in the right direction, then.'

'Yes. And it seems our dragon here wants to be rescued.'

Soon, they come upon a large chamber where all the sewer pipes met.

'This must be the centre of the city,' Zis said.

'But I don't see any… oh.' She spotted the dragon: high above them, suspended in the air with its legs chained to the walls and neck chained to the ceiling. Its wings jetted out into additional chambers either side of the chamber. 'It must be the size of Lastra at least,' she concluded.

'How are we supposed to get up there?!'

'I don't know, maybe we should–'

Then alarm bells started ringing. The Empress' bodyguard surrounded them and finally Empress Ravynne herself entered the chamber, with Ivran by her side.

'Isobys Quorick,' she said. 'Like brother, like sister, eh?'

She dared not look Ivran in the eye. Another traitor. 'Empress.'

'I knew you'd be trouble. And I see you brought our

little rebel along with you. Or did she bring you along?'

'Keep her out of this,' Zis protested.

The Empress turned to Ivran. 'As ever, I thank you for your services, Mr. Oriro.'

He bowed, glancing at Zis as he did so.

'You traitor!' Isobys screamed.

'Now, now,' the Empress said softly, 'there's no need to get emotional about this, is there? You nearly got what you wanted and I'm sure there'll be plenty of time for you to think about why that would have been a very bad thing.'

'We looked in your history books,' Isobys continued. 'You were a member of the council, before they conveniently disappeared. What do you have to say about that?'

'Issy…' Zis warned.

'Oh… Oh! 'Issy' now is it?' the Empress mocked, circling them. 'You just had to make a pet of her, didn't you? You're all the same, you animals. No respect for your betters.' She looked them over, turning her nose up. 'A gnome and a lepus? So unnatural.'

Zis stepped towards her, raising her voice. 'You're a lepus too, you know. Just like me. We're the same species, the same race.'

The Empress shook her head. 'No. No, we're not the same. I've been alive for hundreds of years. I've achieved more than you could possibly imagine you can achieve. I mean, look at you. What are you? Who do you think you are? You're nothing!'

'You ask me who I think I am? Who do you think you are, treating your citizens in this way?'

'I'm Empress Ravynne of Lastra. And if you must know – yes, I was on the council. I was the Elected Representative of the Lepus District. And they – the fools, the stubborn fools! They wouldn't work with me. It was supposed to be equality. Equal treatment, they said! It was equality in servitude – servitude to that beast!' She pointed to the dragon. 'But it wasn't equal. Not for me. They treated me like dirt!'

'So you killed them and seized power for yourself?'

'You talk like it was so simple. Come on. Grow up dear. Surely you must know you won't get anywhere in life with ears like that? They're not sharp enough, not pointy enough. They would never have listened to me.'

'What happened, then?'

'They tried to cut me out of the council. They tried to force me to abdicate. But I refused! I was an elected representative. I served the people of Lastra. So I made a plan for... more equal leadership, so I could serve the Lastran people more equally.'

'But what about now, Empress? What about now? Do you serve the people of Lastra now, with their dragon in the dungeons and their people on the streets?'

'I serve them as they serve me, their Empress.'

'No. No, I don't think they do. They've never faced greater inequality in their lives, in this city's life.'

'Anything is still better than serving that beast.'

'That beast? Oh, yes. The dragon. I think it's time we talk about that. Cideolarth – the Life Giver.'

The Empress scoffed. 'What could you possibly have to say that I haven't already heard? I've heard all the stories. I've seen the truth and I know what it fears. It caved in so easily when it saw I was in control.'

'Gold, yes. It's clever.'

'Your point?'

'Do you know why?'

'What?'

'Why do you think a dragon would be afraid of gold?' Zis asked.

Isobys chuckled to herself.

'What?' the Empress said.

'They breathe fire. They're huge. What do they have to be afraid of?'

'Well–'

'Nothing. Exactly. Now, don't get me wrong, I am by no means a dragon expert. But I'd say they're probably the most powerful living things imaginable. And every story and legend will tell you they're smart. Intelligent. And, more to the point, patient. But one thing they're not, by all accounts, are cowards.'

The Empress couldn't think of anything to say.

'Fear has no purpose to a dragon, wouldn't you think?' she continued. 'It doesn't need to outrun or hide from a predator. It's a dragon. They breathe fire. The elements bend to their will. And I'd bet they could smell a trap from a long way off.'

'What are you saying?' the Empress said, her voice panicked.

Ivran stepped forward. 'I think what the lady is trying to say…'

'Ivran?' the Empress squeaked.

'…is that this dragon here isn't as trapped as you think it is.'

Zis walked towards the Empress, faster now. 'To answer the question, Empress Ravynne… why is a dragon afraid of gold? Because they're smart and they understand the dangers of fire.'

Her eyes widened as the realisation dawned.

'Cideolarth… NOW!' Zis cried.

She grabbed Isobys and they threw themselves to the floor, as the dragon unleashed fire from its throat, engulfing the walls in flames which licked the chambers with one simple stroke.

The walls began to crumble and the chains loosened. Cideolarth tugged and pulled, roaring with each motion to free himself.

Beneath him, Ivran approached the Empress one

last time. 'Shall I give you one last piece of advice, Ravynne?'

'Do I have a choice?' she retorted.

'Surrender,' he said. 'Walk back into the Grand Palace, to the people of your city – who have no doubt heard your wonderful signal of alarm bells by now – and surrender. End this without bloodshed.'

'No.'

He shook his head. 'Ravynne... It doesn't have to end this way.'

'I will never surrender. Not after how you've treated me!'

'You lived a life of privilege, Ravynne, while your city starved. The island floats directionless because you imprisoned its dragon. And yet you still cry foul of your treatment?'

'All my life, it's been like this. People treating me like dirt. Because of who I am.'

'Yes. People do that if you treat them the way you do. It's called equality. But I suppose you could never understand that, could you? Sometimes, people from lives of privilege see inequality in others being treated with the same respect and afforded the same luxuries you are.'

'How dare you speak to your Empress in this way! Ivran, I used to respect you–'

'I used to respect you too, Ravynne. But not

anymore. You see, I look at you now and I don't see a lepus. I don't see a person. I see a husk, a worn-out shell who's been spewing hatred for so long, they've forgotten who they were. They see demons wherever they turn in place of the allies they once had. Yes, I used to respect you, Ravynne – the Ravynne I thought I knew. But I don't know if that Ravynne has been there for a long, long time.'

'Ivran…'

'Don't you think it's time to stop? I'd wager that crown is the only thing keeping you alive right now. What happens if I just… take it off?'

She looked down, contemplating. 'I think you know.'

'Then here's your chance. Accept you were wrong and make things right. Prove to me that maybe there is a Ravynne in there, after all.'

The chamber was crumbling. The chains were nearly loose. Zis looked to Isobys, then to Ivran. 'Ivran! We've got to leave!'

He looked to Ravynne one last time. 'Make your decision. I hope you make the right one.'

Cideolarth finally shook himself loose of the chains, the side walls of the chamber shattering like smashed ice as he swept downwards to land on the ground, curling his wings in front of his rescuers. They climbed on, waiting a second for Ivran to join them and then the dragon set off.

He looked back to see Ravynne, Empress of Lastra, make her last decision. Her eyes searched through her memories, through the years to reach her origin point.

Who did she think she was?

She lifted the crown from her head and waited. The effect would not be immediate but she knew before long the wrinkles would appear and soon enough the last council member from all those years ago would be no more.

The dragon circled the city, stretching his wings for the first time in centuries above the clouds. But the city was falling through the clouds. They could hear the screaming from the city. Chaos had ensued, following the explosion under the Grand Palace. The people had rebelled but the bodyguards were concerned with a far greater danger.

'The city... what's happening?' Isobys asked.

'It's falling!' Ivran said.

'Through the clouds!' Zis contributed.

Cideolarth knew what to do. He thrust his wings up and down and with a sudden lurch downwards thrust himself through the clouds, catching the floating island on his back. And, for the first time in a long while, all was calm in Lastra.

The dragon thrust himself downwards, further still through the cloud layer, until he broke through.

Beneath the ocean, sky was revealed and they gazed upon the forgotten world for the first time.

Isobys turned to Zis, a huge grin plastered across her face. What a view! They just looked at each other and to Ivran, unable to believe their eyes.

They'd done it.

From the clouds, high above the High Wilds, the Elven settlements of Silane and Waque and the forest of the Wisu, which was said to be home to dragons, came into view of an island. Above the Slay Waterways, this land steered a new course through the sky. The gnomes of Kai Darl stopped and ventured out as far as they dared to in the bright sun, to look up and see this forgotten land come to light. The witches trained at Ceat, the purveyors of magical knowledge, ceased their studies to discover something new, as did the lepus' of Tuskbane. In Fogvalor, a mutual haven for all races, their forgotten knowledge of this mighty island named Lastra would be rewritten and forgotten no more.

High above the clouds, this slab of rock still sailed through the skies, control of its direction regained. It would take time to rebuild and time for all to adjust to its new place in the sky. But there would be plenty of time for that – there'd be plenty of time to explore these forgotten worlds.

Deep within the Tree
by Kevin Peake

When one thing goes wrong, there is bound to be another thing to follow.

The city of Sal is built around the birthplace of magic. The Great Tree of Life is believed to be the birthplace of all the races. Since then, the tree has mainly been a symbol of peace to the people of our world. The city has miraculously managed to avoid the war of the races and the subsequent wars which followed.

The war of the races pitted the maikong's and drac's against the elves and lepus'. Even though two hundred years have passed since the last war, hatred between races is still volatile in some places. However, Sal is a place where those seeking to change the story between the races can start anew.

Being a maikong means I was born and raised in

the High Wilds, a city which feels more natural to me. Unfortunately, since I saved the life of a lepus, I have been banished and shamed upon, which is why I ventured to Sal.

Luckily, I didn't make the trip alone. Nami, the lepus I saved, travelled with me to Sal. It took us over six months to cross through the Wild Land, spending most nights sleeping without shelter. We were picked up by a caravan of pilgrims on their way to Sal. Since then, we have hired a room in a local inn and are living the days as they come. However, being a maikong means no one really trusts me which makes it hard to find work.

'Hey, Sammy.' The squeaky voice who was calling me was Nami. Her long grey ears were stood up and her brown eyes were twinkling with the reflection of the light breaking through the trees around us.

'What did I tell you? I don't like the name Sammy or Sam. Either use my name or don't say anything at all.' I could hear the growl in my own voice. She knows I am not a fan of nicknames, yet she will use them to get on my nerves.

'Samantha, have you heard the rumours going around?'

'No. What makes you…' I turn around to see her grubby paws on my tail. She does this as a way to shut me up. 'Ouch!'

'Apparently some people who live close to the tree have been hearing some strange noises at night.' She releases my tail and I can see some of the thick brown hairs fall to the ground. 'Sorry, looks like I grabbed a bit too hard this time.'

'I'm sure it is just the wind.' Grabbed a bit too hard, she's lucky I can't grab hold of that bush she calls a tail. Even if it was long enough for me to grab a hold of, I am sure someone would call out racial abuse and have me in the stocks for a couple of days.

When we first arrived here, I ended up in the stocks for a couple of days because the people here thought I forced Nami to join me on my travels. It took her several days of pleading with the villagers to get them to stop. By that point, I had already had several rotten Alda fruits collide with my face. The red juices stained my canines for several days and the rotten smell took several washes down in the local stream to get rid of.

The only perks to being a maikong is our speed and the height we can jump.

'Wind? do you really think I would be telling you about it if I thought it was just wind?' I can tell that what I said has annoyed her, her whiskers are twitching and her ears won't sit still. 'There is something very strange about it.'

'So, what are you thinking?' I know she has some kind of plan. Lepus are normally shy by nature but not this one. She's wild and just can't keep herself out of trouble.

I look up and down the empty street. Most of the citizens of Sal are down by the river at this time of day. Little homes were carved into the trees surrounding us.

'Ah, you saw through it did you? I was thinking we should stay outside the tree tonight.' As if on cue, not even trying to lie to me, she caves in and tells me.

'You have got to be kidding me. You know they don't like people camping outside.' I pause as I notice she starts doing that thing with her eyes. It makes her seem adorable and you just can't say no to her when she is like that. 'You really think there is something to this?'

'No, not really but, well it can't hurt to find out. Can it?'

Nami was determined to see what was going on and being the protective character that I am, I couldn't let her camp out on her own. Looks like she had roped me into another one of her crazy schemes.

For the rest of the day, we went around Sal, going from one person to another trying to gather information on what was going on with the tree. Everyone we spoke to had the same thing to say. It was just the wind.

Despite the fact that people around here don't want you camping outside, we were going to spend the night camped up on the ground outside the tree. It's not like we haven't camped outside before because on our travel here we would often sleep in the woods or beside the river.

The streets of Sal were different at night. Flamed torches hung outside people's doors, lighting the streets for those who enjoy the night life. This was mainly a time for maikong's and drac's to party without getting in the way of the other races. Myself, I'm a little different. I don't like to party. I'm more of a day maikong and I hang around with Nami. So, even if I wanted to party, my own race wouldn't allow me to party with them.

It just doesn't make sense. After two hundred years, things should be different. We should be allowed to be friends with another race without being disowned by our pack. The rules of the maikong pack are ancient and outdated.

'Samantha,' Nami's voice snaps me out of my thoughts which is probably a good thing. Thinking about my old family brings out the wild beast inside of me.

'What is it?' I answer, not totally aware of the bitterness in my voice.

'Can you hear it?'

I paused and listened closely. There it was, howling, coming from the tree. I looked up but nothing seemed out of the ordinary with it. We waited and there it was again, the wind. It howled from the tree and was carried down through the streets of Sal.

The flames down the streets vanished, one at a time, extinguished by the wind. Darkness had crept up on us quicker than I thought it would. Our eyes were adapted for the dark but mainly using them in daylight has made our night vision difficult to use.

Another howl of wind came from the tree. This time it carried something with it. My fur became damp and cold. I looked over at Nami. Her fur was covered with flecks of water. An overpowering stench of raw flesh burnt my nose. My vision became clouded and Nami faded from view.

'Sammy, are you still there?'

'Yes. Let me find you.'

I reached out with my paw in search for Nami, which brushed across something furry. But the fur was rougher than Nami's and left a sticky residual over my paw.

The dirt beneath me began to move, scratching off the bark beside me. It was followed by a veracious sound, which echoed through my ears and vibrated the trees around me. It was different to before. It came from whatever I was touching.

'What was that?' Nami's voice was weak and sounded far away.

I didn't want to reply, I could still feel that thing. It hadn't moved.

'Samantha, are you there?' I can't stay quiet anymore, she's going to get herself killed.

'Nami, be quiet and keep still.' I whispered to her, hoping she'd listen.

Something was moving the dirt behind me. I turned to try and see what was there in the mist. That was when I noticed the creature I had been touching was gone.

My hand was still covered in the sticky substance from the mysterious creature. That was when I got the first proper chance to smell it. Blood. But who's blood?

The shuffling was getting further away from where we were. I took this chance to try and get close to Nami. I crept across the frost covered dirt floor, to where I last saw her.

Light from the moon had finally began to break through the thick mist.

I found Nami covered in a thin layer of ice. Vapours of her breath escaped from her mouth. I sat down beside her and watched the figures in the mist move away.

'Sam…'

'Keep still and keep quiet. That's all we can do.'

Her voice was barely audible. All I could do was comfort her until we were safe. But, the feeling of safety was slowly fading from my mind, as the faint sounds of screams came from the homes around us. I pulled her close to me and waited.

Shaded figures moved around the mist in front of us. They were more wild than any of the known races. The creatures dragged heavy loads behind them, back into the tree.

I froze in place. Something had my whiskers on edge.

I could feel the creature above me.

A cold, wet drip, splattered onto my face. My eyes looked upwards to see the red eyes form in the shadow.

It had come for us.